NOT POUNDED BY ANYTHING

Six Platonic Tales Of Non-Sexual Encounters

CHUCK TINGLE

CONTENTS

NOT POUNDED IN THE BUTT BY ANYTHING AND THAT'S OKAY

I roll out of a mess of blankets and pillows, clearing my mind as I shake away the sleep and let the warm morning sunlight soak in though my skin. It's a new day.

Next, I take a shower and get dressed, then pour myself a bowl of cereal with chocolate milk; all part of the usual routine. Today feels like just another day in a series of many, but little do I know how important this particular day is about to become.

I check my watch as I head out the door for work, thankful I've carved out enough time to prepare for my big presentation today. Everyone in the office is on pins and needles, but I feel like I've got everything under control.

The first sign that something's not right is when I step from the elevator of my apartment building's massive, hollow car garage, noticing immediately that damn near all the vehicles are missing. Only a handful of cars remain, meaning one of two things: I'm either very late, or everyone else has decided to leave very early.

I check my watch again, just to make sure, then smile confidently. Seven in the morning.

Heading towards my car I suddenly stop, panic shooting through my veins in an icy bolt. I frantically pull the phone from my pocket and check the time, gasping aloud when I see that it's actually eight, not seven, and the device has updated itself automatically.

I forget about the change in daylight savings time.

"Oh fuck," I blurt, suddenly breaking into a sprint as throw open my car door and climb inside.

I peel out from my spot and blast from the garage, weaving my way through the city streets as I struggle to make up lost minutes. While I still might make it to the office in time for my presentation, it's not a guarantee, and I certainly can't prepare in the way I was expecting to.

My heart slamming hard in my chest, I focus intently on the road ahead, my concentration only broken when a brilliant flash of red and blue lights appears in my rearview mirror.

"No!" I cry, immediately realizing what's happening.

I pull my car over to the side of the road and take a deep breath, struggling to think of any way I can get out of this quickly and easily.

A large, muscular unicorn police officer appears at the driver's side window next to me, prompting me to roll it down as I gaze up at him. The creature is shirtless, showing off his perfectly sculpted chest and abs.

"Unicorn Butt Cops: Highway Patrol," the objectively handsome unicorn says in a deep, gruff voice. "Do you know how fast you were going back there?"

I hesitate, not quite sure how to respond. "I *might* have been going a little bit over the speed limit," I finally admit.

The unicorn chuckles to himself, shaking his head as he gazes at me knowingly from behind enormous, mirrored glasses. "You we're going twenty five over. That's pretty fast."

I let out a long sigh. "I'm sorry," I finally say.

The Unicorn Butt Cop nods. "License and registration," he continues.

I hand the officer both, but before he walks away I call out to stop him. "Please!" I shout, prompting the muscular creature to turn around and stroll back to me. "Is there *anything* I can do to speed this process up? Anything at all?"

The unicorn gazes over the rim of his glasses, a single bead of sweat forming on his brow in the brilliant morning sun.

"There is... one thing," the muscular Unicorn Butt Cop replies.

I swallow hard. "Yeah?"

The creature hesitates for a moment. "You can promise to never do it again," he finally says.

"Sounds great!" I reply, thankful to be let off so easy this time.

The Unicorn Butt Cop tears up a blank citation in his hand, then raps twice on the side of my car with his knuckles as he walks away. "Don't do that again, okay? It's dangerous."

"I won't! I promise!" I call out as I start my car and pull onto the city street once more, this time at a respectable speed.

While my presentation is incredibly important, it's certainly not worth getting into an accident over. And besides, even if I *do* manage to make it where I'm going safely, a promise is a promise. I told this Unicorn Butt Cop I'd follow the speed limit, and that's exactly what I intend to do.

Surprisingly, thanks to the fact that most people are already where they need to be and the morning traffic is relatively clear, I arrive at my office building only fifteen minutes later than expected.

I hop out of my ride and grab my briefcase, running over to the elevator and somehow making it inside before the sliding doors close. I press the button for the twenty-third floor and then count down the seconds as my lift cruises upward. It feels so much slower than usual.

The second the doors slide open I'm rushing out into the lobby, heading straight for the conference room where I'm certain everyone else is already waiting.

Seconds later, I'm bursting through the doors to see that I'm absolutely correct, an entire tableful of coworkers immediately turning to look at me. My boss, Mr. Blonto, is at the head of the long conference room table.

Mr. Blonto, a well-dressed bigfoot with dark brown fur and striking blue eyes, furrows his brow when he sees me. "Ken, we weren't sure if you were planning on showing up for your presentation or not."

"I'm so sorry," I apologize, walking to the front of the room as opening up my briefcase. I pull out my notes and make sure everything is where it should be. "I forgot to change my clock."

Mr. Blonto settles back into his chair, clearly a little bothered but not letting it ruin his day. "Fine, fine," the muscular bigfoot tells me, waving his hand in the air as if to push away any lingering thoughts on the matter. "You're here now, what have you got for us?"

I nod, walking over to my projector and flipping it on. "Tingleland," I say aloud as a massive aerial map of the fantastical amusement park appears on the screen behind me. "An enormous theme park for adults, based on the complete works of Dr. Chuck Tingle."

Mr. Blonto's expression doesn't seem to change at all, which gives me great concern, but I push ahead anyway.

"The themepark is going to feature several rides, all of them based on various notable works from Dr. Chuck Tingle. We're going to have rollercoasters, dark rides, virtual reality simulations; the works. More importantly, we're going to have restaurants and, of course, plenty of merchandise."

Mr. Blonto can't help but smile as the sweet mention of merchandising rolls across his ears. It's a reaction that couldn't come soon enough, and the second that I see his stoic façade break I can feel all of my trepidation slip away.

"We're going to have four themed lands within the park," I explain, walking over to the projection and pointing to each of the four segments. "Each one is themed after a different kind of Tingler. We've got Unicornland, Living Objectland, Dinosuarland, and of course, Bigfootland."

My boss is nodding along now, and thusly, his table full of kiss asses are following suit, acting incredibly excited about this idea as it unfolds before them. To be honest, I don't care if their reaction is genuine or not, I'm just glad to have them along for the ride.

"Do you have any questions so far?" I ask Mr. Blonto.

My boss considers this for a moment, letting everything I've just hit him with sink in as he rolls it around in his head.

"You said this is a theme park for adults, right?" Mr. Blonto questions. I nod.

"Chuck Tingle's books are great, I think we can all agree with that, but they're also packed with graphic sex. You can't just have a themepark full of rampant sexual imagery, even if it *is* for adults only."

"Not every Chuck Tingle book has sex in it," I explain.

Mr. Blonto scoffs. "Somehow I doubt that," the well-dressed bigfoot retorts.

"It's true," I insist. "This one isn't."

My boss mulls over these comments a little longer and then, suddenly, makes an announcement to the room. "Alright everyone, get out. Me and Ken need to chat privately for a moment."

My coworkers stand up from their seats and take off without a word, getting back to work like good little drones while Mr. Blonto and I wait silently. Soon enough, the whole room is completely empty other than the two of us.

"May I speak openly?" my boss suddenly questions, a strange request from such an otherwise forward Sasquatch.

"Of course," I tell him, turning off the projector.

Mr. Blonto climbs to his feet and begins to walk slowly towards me, loosening up his tie as he goes and then pulling it off completely.

"I have some concerns about the sexual element of this park," he informs me in a deep, confident tone. "I think I might need a few examples of how it's going to work."

"I *have* a few examples right here," I explain to Mr. Blonto, the hulking bigfoot now standing directly before me.

"I'm gonna need more than that," he retorts, hesitating for a moment. "I'm gonna need… a lot more."

"Anything," I tell him.

Mr. Blonto nods. "I'm gonna need ten ride designs on my desk tomorrow morning. Bright and early"

My boss reaches out his hand and gives me a firm shake. "Great presentation. Why don't you head home and get started on those. I know you're much more creative out of the office."

"Thank you!" I reply. "That's very understanding!"

"No problem," retorts Mr. Blonto, turning and heading for the door. "Looking forward to it!" he calls back over his shoulder.

I collect my things, carefully packing up my briefcase as the excitement overwhelms me. I'd known this idea was a hard sell, but as a lifelong buckaroo I just had to give it a shot. Thankfully, it seems like the rest of my coworkers are, at least, receptive to the concept. Now I just need to blow them away with an incredible collection of ride plans.

I head back to the elevator and make my way down towards the garage once more, my mind already flooded with a myriad of different concepts for Chuck Tingle based rides.

Mr. Blonto was right, I really *am* much more creative when I work from home. I'm even more creative, however, when I work from the library.

With this in mind, I change course and head directly to the nearest library branch I can find.

I pull my car up out front and then head inside, immediately overwhelmed by a powerful sense of relaxation and tranquility as my vision is filled with stacks and stacks of beautiful old books.

In the day of the internet, this place may not be as popular as it once was, but it's just as beautiful as ever.

I stroll over to a nearby table and consider claiming my spot, but at the last second I alter course and decide to go check out any texts there might be regarding theme park history an construction. Maybe there's something laying around here that can get my creative juices flowing.

I know this particular library pretty well, and instinctively head over to the appropriate second. I slowly make my way through the aisles, my eyes wandering over binding after binding as I stroll. There's so much here to get excited about that it's almost overwhelming, and this proves to be the case when I suddenly find myself running directly into another person while they make their way down the aisle across to me.

"I'm so sorry," I blurt, watching as a stack of books that was once held in this person's arms goes clattering to the ground.

I bend down and immediately start gathering the texts, then stand up to find that I'm face to face with a light green raptor in thick-rimmed glasses. The two of us smile immediately as our eyes meet, a powerful sense of friendship and appreciation passing back and forth between us.

"It's okay," the dinosaur tells me. "My fault."

I laugh. "No way, that was totally my fault. I should've been watching where I was going."

"It's fine, it's fine," the raptor continues to assure me.

I notice now that this prehistoric creature is shirtless, but he wears an official library nametag attached to the waistband of his pants.

"Oh, you work here," I stammer.

The dinosaur nods. "I'm Trip, the handsome Jurassic librarian."

"It's nice to meet you Trip! I'm Ken," I inform him. "I was actually looking for some books on the history of famous amusement parks."

The raptor smiles. "Well, I'm glad I can help you then. We've been doing some rearranging. The history section is over *there* now," he explains, pointing a long, clawed finger across the library.

"Thank you so much," I gush.

The dinosaur casually leans against a nearby bookshelf now, his eyes narrowing slightly. "Is there anything else I can help you with?" he coos.

I consider his words for a moment. There's something very cool about this raptor that I can't quite put my finger on, a confident demeanor that makes me want to spend more time with him.

"What are you doing after work?" I finally question. "I've got a lot to do before my big meeting tomorrow, but if I get it finished then maybe we could hang out and talk about libraries."

"Are you sure?" Trip questions. "I don't wanna interrupt your work."

"Oh yeah," I assure him. "Some people think it's best to work and work and work before a big meeting like this, but what they don't realize is how important it is to relax, as well. You've gotta take care of your business, of course, but you can't over do it."

Trip grins with his perfect rows of sharp dinosaur teeth. "I think I can help you relax," he says. "I'll see you tonight."

I've just finished plating dinner when the doorbell rings, and I walk over with both excitement and apprehension. I can already tell that Trip is a very, very hip dinosaur, and I hope that he thinks I'm just as hip in return.

I open the door. "Hey! Come in!" I offer my new friend.

The muscular raptor strolls inside, still shirtless. He glances around my apartment and nods in appreciation of my interior decorating skills. "This is a great place," Trip tells me.

"Thank you," I reply.

I can tell now that there's a powerful tension blossoming between us, a potent ache that I can't quite put my finger on but simmers with intensity in the pit of my stomach. It builds and builds as the two of us stand here in silence, just staring at one another until, eventually; I realize exactly what this feeling is.

"I'm so fucking hungry," I suddenly blurt. "I'm sorry, I should've had a bigger lunch. I know you just got here but can we have dinner now?"

"Yes," the muscular raptor gushes. "Of course."

Suddenly, we're rushing over to the dinner table, taking our seats and immediately chowing down on the food before us. I open wide and take a huge spoonful of mashed potatoes into my mouth, savoring the sweet, buttery flavor while I gaze across the table at my new friend. Trip is clearly enjoying himself, too, lost in a moment of utter satisfaction as he tries the green beans.

"Fuck. This is so fucking good," the dinosaur groans.

"Thank you," I moan in reply. "I'm proud of how it turned out."

I shovel more and more of the delicious food into my mouth,
alternating between the potatoes and the beans until, finally, I just can't take
it anymore and take both between my lips at the same time. I swallow
hungrily, taking the strange mess of flavors down my throat as I close my
eyes tight and focus on the sensation. It's honestly much better than I
would've thought, and only adds to the confident assertion that I've done a
pretty good job for an amateur cook.

Now it's time for the main course, but despite how excited I am, I
can't help but hesitate.

"You seem nervous," Trip informs me.

I nod. "I am."

"Why?" he coos.

"I've never done this before," I finally admit.

Trip looks shocked. "Cooked?"

"Not for a guest like this," I continue. "Mashed potatoes and green
beans are easy, but I don't know how I did on the main dish."

"I'm sure it's fine," the muscular, shirtless dinosaur assures me.

I stand up and stroll over to the kitchen, peeking into the oven and
then glancing back over my shoulder at the raptor. It certainly *looks*
amazing, but who knows how this roast actually tastes.

Slowly, I open the over farther and farther until it's gaping wide for
Trip to see, the sizzling main course looking absolutely mouthwatering as it
waits for me and the raptor to make our move.

"You like what you see?" I call back to the dinosaur, his eyes
transfixed on the delectable treat before him.

"Fuck yeah," Trip offers in return.

I take a deep breath, then let it out, trying my best to collect myself
before taking a final leap into the unknown.

"I have to tell you something," I say, my voice trembling slightly.

"What is it?" Trip questions, a look of grave concern making its way
across his face.

"This isn't meat, it's vegetarian," I finally inform him. "I hope that's
okay."

I hold my breath, on pins and needles as I wait for the librarian
raptor's reply. His expression stays completely blank for much longer than
I'd like, but eventually a grin begins to creep its why across his lips.

"I've never had a vegetarian roast," he says. "Sounds exciting! What's in it?"

"I'm not sure," I admit. "I just got it at the store. Pea protein I think?"

The raptor climbs up from his seat and positions himself behind me, leaning over my shoulder as he smells the delicious roast. He takes a big sniff, holding it in for a minute and then letting it out slowly. In and out the dinosaur breathes, quickly falling into a rhythm with me as we analyze this exciting new addition to our meal.

"Fuck yeah," the shirtless dinosaur gushes. "That smells like a roast to me. I can't even tell the difference."

"Wanna help me get it out?" I ask.

Trip nods and soon enough the two of us are pulling the sizzling faux meat dish out of the oven, setting it on the kitchen counter and admiring the bubbling juices that swim around it in the pan. I reach into a nearby drawer and pull out a large knife, cutting off a thick slab for each of us before we return to our seats at the table.

"I can't wait for this," the dinosaur says, his eyes wide and his mouth watering.

Without hesitation we dive in, consuming the main course with a blissed out fervor unlike anything I've experienced. Sharing this moment with my new friend is incredible, and the pleasure of the meal is only elevated by his presence.

Now the two of us are moaning and groaning together, losing ourselves in the moment as we chow down on our succulent roasts. Trip plunges his fork into the slab of tender juiciness over and over again, starting slowly at first and then picking up speed as the flavors overwhelm him.

Not wanting to be left behind, I quickly fall into a rhythm behind Trip, eating at his pace as I continue to shovel more food into my body. Faster and faster we go, until eventually I'm worried there will soon be no roast left.

Of course, that's when I remember I've got a whole tray of the sizzling goodness left to be devoured.

"More?" I question.

"Fuck yeah, more," the shirtless dinosaur grunts enthusiastically.

I take our plates, which are now wiped completely clean, then head back into the kitchen for another helping of this incredible meal. This time, I slice off two even larger hunks of the roast, not slowing down for a second.

I take a spoon and ladle on some of the juices around it, making sure everything is nice and wet, then return to the table and set my handiwork before Trip once more.

"It's all yours," I tell him.

I watch in awe as the dinosaur continues to wolf down the delicious roast, putting my worries of a vegetarian menu completely to rest as he slams the food down his through in a state of aching, belligerent passion.

The dinosaur has consumed his entire second slab before I even sit down, which causes me to reel in shock.

Trip notices this and quickly apologizes. "Oh my god, I'm so sorry. Was that too fast?"

"No," I assure him, shaking my head with a wry smile plastered across my face. "I like it. Actually, I fucking love it."

I take the shirtless, muscular creature's plate and carry it back to the kitchen, loading it up with more and more of the roast before returning to Trip.

Of course, the hungry dinosaur promptly wolfs it down once more.

This process goes one for quite a while, in and out of the kitchen for what seems like forever until it feels like the dinosaur is about to reach his breaking point.

"Oh my god," Trip groans. "I'm so stuffed, I think I'm gonna blow."

"Wait!" I cry out. "Just one last thing."

I run back to the kitchen, but this time I don't go for the roast, which is nothing but scraps by now. Instead, I head to the freezer and open it up, pulling out a sweet and frozen tub of delicious ice cream. I prepare us two large bowls of the velvety goodness and then carry them over to my friend, setting one down before him and another one in front of myself.

"Think you've got room?" I question playfully.

"I've got this," the dinosaur assures me.

The next thing I know we're both diving into the ice cream with a ravenous hunger, swallowing massive spoonfuls of the milky liquid. I don't even stop to wipe my chin as the white liquid rolls down my face in long, thick streaks, dangling in the air before dripping off into the bowl once more.

Of course, I'm determined to finished it all, and I immediately get to work scooping up the remainder of the ice cream. I swallow the milky thickness with hunger and passion, utterly beside myself as the sweetness overwhelms me.

"Fuck," I finally moan, collapsing back into my chair. "That was amazing."

"You're telling me," the raptor chimes in, looking equally satisfied.

We sit like this for a while before Trip stands up and strolls over, rounding the table and taking a seat in the chair next to me instead of across. There's something about this closeness that I like, as though I can physically sense the way that my new friend is starting to open up to me.

"I was thinking," the dinosaur begins. "I really like you, and I'd love it if we spent more time together."

"I like you, too," I tell him.

Suddenly, the raptor reaches out and touches my arm in a way that I'm not quite prepared for, breaking past the boundaries of a friendship and ending up somewhere else entirely. I pull back slightly, which fills Trip's expression with grave concern.

"I'm sorry," the dinosaur offers.

"It's okay," I assure him. "I'm just... not interested in anything physical."

Trip considers this a moment. "That's okay, we can just be friends."

I shake my head. "No, no. I don't mean it like that... we can *definitely* be more than friends, but I'm never going to be interested in having sex. If you're okay with that, then so am I. If not, I totally understand."

"I'm interested," the muscular raptor says with a smile. "So what does that make us? Buds? Boyfriends?"

I shrug, laughing as I realize what an understanding and caring companion I've found. "I don't know yet, but it's all on the table. I just can't wait to figure it out together."

NOT POUNDED IN THE BUTT BY MY BOOK "NOT POUNDED IN THE BUTT BY ANYTHING AND THAT'S OKAY" AND THAT'S OKAY

I love Billings, but I'll be damned if it doesn't feel good to get out of town for a while. During these cold winter months, most of my time is spent indoors with my family; watching TV, gathered around the dinner table, or working on new books. As an author, I absolutely love to get cozy and warm, curled up on the couch with a pen and a notepad as I sketch out my plans for a new Dingler.

Dingler, of course, is a term that I've coined for one of my erotic short stories, a tale so sensual that it makes you feel a slight dingle in your stomach. This type of romantic literature has served me well, and by now most people in the publishing world are well aware of the name Luck Dingle.

Suffice to say, I'm a pretty busy guy.

Recently, the business aspect of my life has become just a bit too overwhelming, and with the publication of my new hit book, Not Pounded In The Butt By Anything And That's Okay, there's little room for much else.

My son, Ron, who I live with, has noticed the stress that I'm under, and finally suggested something that had not once crossed my mind since I started writing Dinglers.

Maybe it's time for a well-deserved vacation. No ice, no cold, no annoying neighbor Todd Kibbler getting in my face every day.

This is how I ended up finding my seat here in a massive jumbo jet, fueled up and ready to disembark on its long journey from Billings to Hawaii.

Despite the fact that I'll miss my family over the course of this week, I'm absolutely buzzing with excitement, thrilled to finally see this incredible island for myself. Truth be told, I'm also pretty excited about the open seat next to me, and with only a few minutes left until the plane doors close for good, it looks like I'm in for a comfortable flight with plenty of space to stretch out.

I pull out the inflight menu, flipping through to see if they offer any spaghetti or chocolate milk with the meal service. Of course, second's later someone is tapping me on the shoulder and pointing to the seat next to me.

"I'm over there," comes a deep voice.

I glance up and begin to stand, then halt abruptly when I see who it is.

"Oh my god!" I gasp. "This is so crazy."

There before me is the sentient manifestation of my own book, Not Pounded In The Butt By Anything And That's Okay. Huge smiles immediately cross our faces as we hug, then I move out of the way to let him pass, the giant living book taking his seat by the window.

"What are you doing here?" I gush.

"Just, thought I could use a vacation," my book tells me with a smile. "What about you?"

"Same," I admit with a nod. "Guess we really are cut from the same cloth."

"You *did* write me," Not Pounded In The Butt By Anything And That's Okay offers, causing me to chuckle knowingly.

My book continues to smile but, at this point, I notice something strange about his expression, a slight falter that I wasn't quite expecting. If anything, this book should be overflowing with excitement, he *is* a bestseller after all, but instead he just seems to be going through the motions. Not Pounded In The Butt By Anything And That's Okay is being polite and patient as he makes his way through the day, but nothing more.

"Are you sure you're fine?" I question. "You can tell me, you know that, right?"

The living book lets out a long sigh. "I've just been so overwhelmed lately. It's a lot to take one for someone who has only existed a few days."

I'd never considered that , but Not Pounded In The Butt By Anything And That's Okay has a great point. Before I wrote him, there was nothing, but now my book has suddenly been thrust into existence with all eyes on him. He hasn't been able to carve out an identity for himself yet.

"I'm sorry," I finally offer with a nod of understanding.

"It's a strange thing to start off famous, to have everyone wondering who you really are even though you don't quite know it for yourself," the sentient object continues. "I just had to get away for a minute and figure some things out… to understand what being asexual means to *me*."

"Oh," I blurt. "That's something I didn't even consider. I mean, you don't *have* to take on the subject of your pages. It's your choice. I know plenty of scary stories who aren't actually frightening once they've manifested as living books. Hell, I've even met a cookbook who couldn't cook to save his life."

"Not this time," Not Pounded In The Butt By Anything And That's Okay says firmly. "If there's one thing I know, it's that sex doesn't interest me at all. I don't think it ever will."

I smile and nod. "Well, I'm not gonna pretend to know what it means to be a living book who has only existed for a few days and is learning his sexuality, or lack of sexuality, but I want you to know that I'm here for you if you ever want to talk. I respect you so much, and from author to book… I'm so damn proud of you."

"Thanks," Not Pounded In The Butt By Anything And That's Okay replies.

There's a moment of silence between us and then the sentient book turns to face forward again, putting on his headphones and tuning me out.

Suddenly, a loud roar erupts from beneath the plane, the engines howling as we gradually speed up. The vessel is moving faster and faster now, hurtling forward until, finally, there's nowhere left to go but up. The next thing I know, we're taking off into the sky, headed on a direct course for paradise.

The resort I'm at is absolutely breathtaking, tropical flowers and vines hanging from every inch of this otherwise modern hotel at the water's edge, white sandy beaches just seconds away from the hotel lobby. From my room I can see the entire bay, watch as the waves pulse back and forth across the shore while playful vacationers swim and splash in the water.

I've only been here for a few hours and I'm already on a steady diet of fresh fruits, taking in all of the succulent flavors of the island. I can't want for dinner later, for which I've managed to get a killer reservation, but until then I plan on taking a stroll along the water and letting the island vibes overwhelm my senses.

It's time to relax.

I throw on my shorts and head out onto the bench, closing my eyes and enjoying the way that the wet sand slides through my toes. The water is lapping softly around my ankles, gently pulling back and forth across my skin.

When I open my eyes again, I find my gaze drawn to the silhouettes of surfers as they glide across the waves. Everyone seems to be having the time of their lives out there; instructors giving lessons, whole gangs of friends racing across the top of a swell and then charging down the other side.

Only one long figure seems to not be enjoying himself.

I put my hand over my eyes, trying to squint past the beams of sunlight to make sense of the rectangular shape that sits completely motionless atop his board, deep in thought.

Just as I suspected, it's Not Pounded In The Butt By Anything And That's Okay.

"Hey!" I call out, waving enthusiastically. "Of all the places to end up on this island, we're here on the same beach! First the plane and now this, kinda crazy right?"

My living books shrugs. "No, not really. This is definitely not some romance novel where serendipity brings us together."

"Oh, okay," I stammer. "I just meant that it's nice to see you again."

"Nice to see you, too," the sentient book calls back over the rolling waves.

"Maybe we could surf together later," I suggest. "I've never been, but I want to learn."

Not Pounded In The Butt By Anything And That's Okay shakes his head. "I don't think so," he tells me. "No offense or anything, I just think I should be alone. Surfing lessons could turn romantic pretty quick and I'm asexual, remember?"

"Uh... I don't think that's how it works," I call back, "but I respect your decision!"

The living book nods and then turns his attention elsewhere, just sitting on his board and staring out across the waves in silence while the sun creeps its way across the sky.

With nothing else to say, I continue making my way down the beach, exploring the beautiful island setting as it unfurls around me.

For a brief moment I consider letting Not Pounded In The Butt By Anything And That's Okay on a secret of my own, but then decide against it.

He's got this.

The host leads me over to my table, an incredible spot on the edge of the patio that looks out across the vast ocean cove below. In the distance the sun has just started to set, barely touching the edge of the volcanic mountain crater that brings this gorgeous vista to life.

I pull out my menu and scan down the list of incredible looking seafood, from soft shell crab to fresh caught mahi mahi. My mouth is watering just thinking about it, and I'm so distracted by the thought of this delicious meal that I don't even notice Not Pounded In The Butt By Anything And That's Okay making his way through the restaurant.

It's only when he sits down two tables away from me that the book and I lock eyes, exchanging a brief nod before the sentient collection of words turns his attention elsewhere. He's going well out of his way to avoid me now.

Of course, I can't help but notice that we're the only two people here sitting alone, and while I'm completely fine with this fact, the sentient book's body language makes me suspicious that he's not.

For a brief moment I consider inviting him over to sit with me, but then stop myself when I remember his previous words. This is a short story that has been firm in his desire to be left alone.

As I watch Not Pounded In The Butt By Anything And That's Okay, however, he begins to relax, a slight change of expression overwhelming his face as he begins to consider his options. Eventually, the living book gives in completely, his gaze returning to mine as he smiles apologetically.

The sentient collection of pages stands up and walks over to my table. "Mind if I join you?" he asks with deep sincerity.

I nod. "Of course! I thought you'd never ask!"

Now Pounded In The Butt By Anything And That's Okay takes the seat across from me, looking as though a heavy weight has been lifted off his shoulders. "I'm sorry about the way I've been acting," he offers. "It's just... I've only existed for a few days and there's so much to sort out."

"It's okay," I reply, nodding in agreement. "Learning who you are can take time. Sometimes it's instant and you understand yourself from the very beginning, but sometimes it can take days, weeks, years, or an entire lifetime; and that's fine! There are no rules about how _you_ get to learn yourself. All you need to know is this: it's okay to be you."

My sentient book smiles.

"For some reason, I felt like I couldn't be asexual _and_ have connections to other people," he continues, laying it all out for me and chuckling at how silly this now seems. "But when I was sitting there at the other table, I suddenly realized there were _no rules_ about who I am. I _can_ be romantic without wanting to have sex. I _can_ love without wanting to have sex. Anyone who says otherwise is... is..."

"A fucking asshole," I chime in.

"Yes!" the living book blurts. "Nobody gets to decide who I am besides me."

"And who are you?" I continue.

Not Pounded In The Butt By My Book And That's Okay considers this for a moment. "Well, I'm still sorting that out, but so far I know that I want love, and I want romance, but I don't want sex, and that's okay."

"Exactly," I reply with a nod.

"Thank you for helping me understand all this," my book offers.

I shake my head. "No, no, no. You figured this out all by yourself. Even though I created you, I'm in no position to tell you who you are, only you can do that."

The waiter suddenly arrives and asks if we've had a chance to look at the menu, to which we both shake our heads but insist that we can order quickly. I glance down and instinctively go for the mahi mahi, which I was eyeing closely, and my book orders the same.

"Both on vacation at the same time," the living collection of words offers with a chuckle as the waiter takes our menus and strolls away. "Both at the same resort; both ordering the mahi mahi. I guess we _do_ have a lot in common."

"Both asexual," I continue, adding one more to the pile.

Not Pounded In The Butt By Anything And That's Okay does a

powerful spit take, the water erupting from his mouth in an enormous plume as he reels in his chair.

"What?" the living story cries out. "You're asexual, too?"

"I am on this timeline," I inform him, "but there are many versions of me across endless layers of reality."

"Uh… What?" is all the sentient books can say.

"Nevermind. Author stuff," I reply, shaking my head and waving away his concern. "The point is, yes, I'm asexual, too."

"What didn't you tell me sooner?" Not Pounded In The Butt By Anything And That's Okay questions. "When I was acting like that earlier you could've just told me how to be!"

"I'm just a writer," I explain. "It's not my job to tell you who to be. There's only one person in the world who knows exactly who you are, and that's you."

The two of us continue talking like this as the sun gradually drifts down behind the distant volcanic crater, slowly transforming the sky above us from dark blue, to purple, and then to a beautiful cascade of luscious pinks and oranges that explode across the scattered clouds.

When the food arrives we dive in hungrily, both of us utterly thrilled by just how delicious the meal is.

There's clearly a connection between Not Pounded In The Butt By Anything And That's Okay and me, and it very well might be romance.

One thing's for sure, though, it's definitely not sexual.

Once we finish up, my living book and me spend the rest of the evening staring out at the enormous, mountainous crater in the distance, watching as it's mammoth form disappears into complete darkness and the stars begin twinkling above.

I can tell that there's something on Not Pounded In The Butt By Anything And That's Okay's mind, an idea that's been rolling around in his head for a while now and filling him with a powerful tension.

Eventually, my book takes a deep breath and then lets it out, making his move.

"Would you like to come back to my place?" he finally questions. "Is that a weird thing to ask?"

I shake my head. "Nope, not weird at all. I mean, I understand that a lot of people use that as a way to hint at sex, but we've already established clear boundaries together."

"Really?" the living book cries out with excitement. "So you'll come over?"

"I'd love that," I tell him.

Soon enough, the two of us have paid our bills and are walking a quiet street lined with tiki torches back to our hotel. We arrive and then head up to the sentient book's room, finally entering and collapsing onto the bed.

"You want to watch a movie?" Not Pounded In The Butt By Anything And That's Okay questions.

"Sure!" I reply, excited for a chance to truly relax in the presence of this kind and caring book.

The two of us settle in and throw on a movie but, to be honest, I can't focus on the story at all. Instead, my mind remains squarely transfixed on just how comfortable I feel here.

We fall asleep like this, basking in the warm glow of each other without an ounce of sexual tension between us.

"Lets go," a familiar voice says, waking me from my slumber.

I glance up to see Not Pounded In The Butt By Anything And That's Okay standing over me, extending a full water bottle for me to take.

I grab the bottle from the living object's hands and take a long swing. "I'm awake. What time is it?"

"Time to get out there and enjoy the island together," the living book tells me. "In a strictly platonic way, of course."

I sit up and rub my eyes, gazing out the window of Not Pounded In The Butt By Anything And That's Okay's room to see that dawn has barely just arrived. Regardless, I'm feeling surprisingly refreshed and ready to go, interesting to see where the day might take us.

I notice now that Not Pounded In The Butt By Anything And That's Okay is wearing shorts and his hiking shoes, ready to head out.

"Where are we going?" I ask.

The living book turns around and points out the window behind him, signaling across a breathtaking vista towards the giant volcanic crater in the distance.

I quickly change my clothes, then the two of us head downstairs and climb into my rental car. The energy between my living book and me is overwhelmingly potent, a sense of fun and adventure that warms me down to the very pit of my soul. It's nice to have a companion like this, someone who's ready to wake up early and seize the day.

"So what are you working on now?" my living book questions as we begin our drive to the hiking trail. "Got any new books you're working on?"

I roll my eyes. "This is supposed to be a vacation, of course I'm not working!"

"Then what do you keep jotting down in that notepad you've got stuffed in your back pocket," Not Pounded In The Butt By Anything And That's Okay questions.

I can't help but laugh, recognizing that I've been caught. "Alright, alright. I told myself I wasn't going to work but I just can't stop it completely."

"Well then," my sentient book continues, glancing over at me. "Out with it."

I let out a long sigh. "Well, if you must know, I've started working on a book called Not Pounded In The Butt By My Book 'Not Pounded In The Butt By Anything And That's Okay' And That's Okay."

"It sounds great!" the living collection of words replies. "What's it about?"

"This," I inform him. "It's literally this."

"Right now?" the living book continues.

I nod. "You can't see the words?" I point out through the windshield in front of me, extending my finger as Not Pounded In The Butt By Anything And That's Okay follows along.

He's squinting as he struggles to see what I'm talking about. "Where?" the living book finally questions. "All I see is the crater. Are the words behind it?"

"More like… through it," I explain. "See how you said 'crater' just now? That created a word on the page of our story, which is being written by Chuck Tingle."

"I'm so lost," the sentient idea admits.

"Just try saying 'crater' again," I offer, "but when you say it, I want you to look for the word itself, not the object. Think about the blank page of this story, and then see what changes when you add to it."

"Crater," Not Pounded In The Butt By Anything And That's Okay states loud and clear. "Oh my god, I see it!"

"Cool, huh?" I offer.

The living book nods. "So... we're just characters in a book?"

I shake my head. "We're characters in a book, but we're not *just* characters in a book. A lot of people are going to read this, and hopefully they'll like it."

Not Pounded In The Butt By Anything And That's Okay lets out a long sigh. "I just hope we can give them what they want."

"Well, Chuck normally writes about pounding butts, and this story is specifically *not* about pounding butts, so that might be a little difficult. It's not impossible, though."

"I'm up for the challenge," Not Pounded In The Butt By Anything And That's Okay replies confidently.

"Here's the thing," I explain. "Normally, Chuck's books end in a very visceral and passionate way, but I think the point of this story is that two people who care about each other can be just as visceral and passionate together with or without sex."

"It's gonna take some serious physical activity to make that work," my living book replies.

"Exactly," I offer with a nod.

Just then, then two of us pull into a parking lot at the base of the crater.

We erupt from the car and immediately head up towards the path, which is clearly marked by an old wooden sign and a single arrow that points up into the lush jungle before us.

By now the morning sun is already beating down, so the shade of this trail comes as a welcome treat. Hiking up through the canyon immediately sends a sharp chill down my spine, the cool night air still lingering here below the overgrowth. Not Pounded In The Butt By Anything And That's Okay and me exchange glances.

"You like that?" my living book questions gruffly.

"I fucking love it," I tell him, continuing upward.

The two of us start off slowly at first, pumping our legs back and forth as we adjust to the incline. This is a formidable hike, but the two of us know what we're doing as we begin our ascent up the side of this absolutely enormous canyon.

It's not long before my sentient book and me fall into a confident rhythm together, our strides locking in as our breathing becomes heavy and labored. Sweat is beginning to collect on my forehead and I wipe it away, pushing myself even harder.

"God damn," I grunt, not used to this kind of workout but refusing to give in to the aching discomfort. "How you feeling?"

"Good, you?" my book replies.

"Okay," I admit. "A little sore. I've just gotta push through it."

"You've got this," Not Pounded In The Butt By Anything And That's Okay replies. "We've both got this, together."

Driven onward by his kind and encouraging words, I push up the trail, my feet planting firm in the dirt as we climb higher and higher. The discomfort that I once felt quickly begins to melt away, replaced instead by a pleasant warmth. I feel as though I'm fully present within my body right now, truly feeling every nerve ending as the adrenaline surges through my system.

"Oh yeah, this is amazing," I gush.

"Faster?" the sentient book questions from behind me.

"I don't know if I can take it but... yeah," I continue. "Let's fucking do it."

The two of us pick up our pace even more until, eventually, we're no longer just climbing up the side of this crater, we're jogging. The dirt slams hard under our feet as we make our way up the side, the dull repetitive thud echoing out across the landscape around us.

"We're almost there, we're almost there," I start repeating as the words tumble out of my mouth over and over again, speaking to myself more than anyone else. With every passing round the mantra grows louder, until eventually I'm crying out at the top of my lungs. "We're almost there!"

Suddenly, I erupt into the sunlight, finding myself on the edge of a massive cliff from which the entire island can be seen in all of its glorious beauty. I turn and discover my sentient book right next to me, immediately flooded with gratitude at the fact that the two of us could overcome this incredible obstacle together. We hug excitedly and then jump up and down a few times, crying out just to hear our howls echoing down the ridge.

"That was amazing," I gush.

"It was, I feel very close to you in a very romantic, but utterly non-sexual way," offers Not Pounded In The Butt By Anything And That's Okay.

"The feeling's mutual," my book assures me.

Suddenly, the living object's expression changes from one of elation to confusion as he stares past me into the great vastness of the ocean. I turn around and follow his gaze, then stop and gasp when I see what he's looking at. It's not like I didn't know it was coming, but that doesn't mean I'm not surprised.

"What *is* that?" the living book questions.

"The blank page," I explain. "That's the end of our story."

As we watch, the vast emptiness sweeps towards us, not black or white, but a strange unknown color that could never truly be defined from here within the story.

"That was a lot of fun," Not Pounded In The Butt By Anything And That's Okay offers. "I'll miss you."

I laugh. "Oh, don't worry, you'll be seeing me again very, very soon."

"I will?" the living object questions.

"Of course," I reply. "Every time someone reads this we'll be back. Our time together may fly by fast, but it's a very important tale. I'm sure they'll be plenty of readers."

The sentient book smiles. "Well, in that case I'll see you soon."

"Can't wait," I offer as the wave of blankness pushes up against me.

It washes across us, leaving nothing more than an empty page and the desire to read this story of love once more.

NOT POUNDED AT THE LAST SECOND BECAUSE CONSET CAN BE GIVEN AND REVOKED AT ANY MOMENT AND THIS IS A WONDERFUL THING THAT'S IMPORTANT TO UNDERSTAND

As the bus rumbles around us I can already feel myself getting nervous, the anxiety and tension within my body finally manifesting itself. I'm staring out through the window at a glorious desert landscape as it passes me by, a flood of questions making their way through my head.

Is white water rafting really as dangerous as it seems?

If everything else is so dry, where's the river?

I could go on and on, but at this point I'm getting so worked up that I decide to turn my attention to anything else, leaning back against my seat and closing my eyes tight.

"Everything okay?" the guy next to me questions.

I open my eyes slightly, making note of the concerned look on my seat companion's face.

"Yeah, I'm fine," I tell him with a slight nod, not quite sure if my expression is as convincing as my words.

"I'm Treen," he offers, shaking my hand.

"Blip," I inform him. "You ever done this before?"

Treen nods. "Plenty of times, it's a lot of fun."

"Really?" I question. "Because I've always wanted to go rafting, but it never really looked all that fun."

"Why go then?" Treen asks me with a chuckle.

"To challenge myself, I guess," I inform my new friend. "It seems dangerous and exciting."

Treen can't help but crack a smile. "It's not as scary as you'd think," he informs me. "It looks much more thrilling than it actually is. I'm not saying rafting is boring, it's not, but those explosions of white water always amp up the visuals."

I take in the man's words, but they still don't change much about my own internal struggles and fears. My new friend can see this, and he tries again.

"Listen, here's the thing about rafting," Treen offers, leaning in close. "Everybody seems to think you don't have any control, that you're on this boat going down the river, and that river is heading we're it's heading no matter what you do."

"That's exactly what it seems like," I reply.

"Well, it's not true. First of all, there are plenty of paths in a river to choose from. Some of those paths are rough and wild, but others are calm and slow and they take their time to wind through the canyon," Treen explains. "Second, you can always just stop and get out of the water."

"I can?" I blurt, this very simple thought never once crossing my mind.

"Of course," Treen continues. "If you're not feeling it, just pull your raft over to the shore and get off. You don't even need a reason, just do it."

Finally, I feel a powerful wave of relaxation wash its way across my body, filling me with a sense of confidence that I never had before. Ironically, this realization that I can stop my rafting trip, should I need to, gives me more than enough inspiration to go through with it.

The bus begins to slow down, pulling off of our main drag through the desert and beginning a winding decent into the canyon below. The air around us immediately becomes cooler through the open windows, lush plants and shrubbery springing up on either side of the road.

Eventually, we pull into a small parking area on the side of a wide, blue river, the water calmly meandering its way through this canyon as it slices a path through this otherwise arid landscape.

"Alright, everybody out!" our bus driver calls from the front. "Don't forget your life jackets."

The bus full of rafters stands in unison as we begin to shuffle out into the beautiful natural setting. Everything here in the canyon seems more vibrant that what I'm used to, the hills a deeper orange, the trees a healthier green, and the water a powerful, brilliant turquoise.

Without further instructions, our small group of rafters begins to chat amongst ourselves, making introductions and struggling to relate after being thrust into this brand new collective. Everyone here comes from a different walk of life, brought together by the simple fact that we all signed up for a beginners white water rafting trip for some reason on another. There are clearly a few people who've done this before, like Treen, but most of the people standing around seem just as nervous as I do.

"Alright, alright!" comes booming voice from down on the riverbank.

Our crowd glances over to see a handsome bigfoot strolling up the bank towards us, his lush brown fur glistening wet from the river. He's muscular, perfectly sculpted with massive arms and a barrel of the chest.

The second that I see this beautiful Sasquatch, I find myself incredible attracted to him, and based on the powerful silence that falls across our crowd, I'm not the only one.

"I'm Garto Grims," the handsome bigfoot announces. "I'll be your guide for today's trip, along with my assistants here."

Garto waves over to a pair of equally muscular men, one of which hands him a paddle.

"How many of you have been white water rafting before?" Garto questions.

A smattering of people raise their hands, including one particularly excited fellow in the front.

"Last time I went, I got lost on the river and met the physical manifestation of Saturday," the man blurts. "I haven't seen him since then, but I'd like to reconnect."

"Unfortunately, that's a different story entirely, that is Saturday Pounds Me In The Butt, and this is Not Pounded At The Last Second Because Consent Can Be Given And Revoked At Any Moment And This Is A Wonderful Thing That's Important To Understand," Garto offers in return. "However, this is a tingler, so you never know what could happen. Now, I'm gonna go through the basics of white water rafting with you. After that, if you still have any questions then I'll try my best to answer them."

Garto continues his safety instructions, but my mind is spinning. I lean over to my new friend, Treen, who is now standing next to me.

"What does he mean this is a *tingler*?" I question. "I don't get it."

"A tingler," Treen repeats back, as though this simple explanation is of some meaning to me.

I continue to stare at him blankly, until finally Treen realizes something and starts chuckling loudly.

"Oh shit, you don't know, do you?" he continues. "I've heard about characters who don't know, but I've never actually met one before. This is great."

"Don't know *what?*" I blurt, getting a little frustrated now.

Treen collects himself a bit, realizing that this conversation is going to be a little more nuanced than he first suspected. He opens his mouth to speak, then halts again, considering another perspective before finally moving forward.

"Do you remember what you were doing before that bus ride?" my new friend questions.

"Of course," I reply. "I was…"

Suddenly my mind goes blank, struggling to recall this simple yet incredibly difficult-to-grasp information.

"I don't know," I finally admit, "but I got on the bus somehow."

"Did you?" Treen questions. "Do you actually remember getting on?"

I begin to reply and then suddenly, to my own horror, realize I have no recollection of this event. As far as I know, I just appeared in my seat at some point during the journey.

"Why can't I remember any of this stuff?" I finally stammer, fear surging through my veins.

"Because it wasn't written," Treen explains. "I know it's a lot to take in, but don't worry. This is all heading somewhere important. Chuck's handling it."

"Who the hell is Chuck? And if he's so great then why can't he calm me down?" I cry out, my voice trembling.

Suddenly, a wave of relaxation flows across me, chilling me out before I take things too far and start drawing attention from the rest of the crowd.

"Better?" Treen questions.

I nod.

"See, we're all characters in a book that Chuck is writing. We're here to tell a story," Treen continues. "That guy over there who raised his hand was already in a tingler, apparently one where he got pounded in the butt by the physical manifestation of Saturday, after a river rafting trip."

"Pounded in the butt?" I blurt. "What kind of book *is* this?"

"Erotica," Treen replies flatly.

I glance over at him, chuckling to myself, then freeze when I notice the man's expression is utterly stoic. "Wait, really?" I question.

Treen nods.

"Am *I* going to get pounded?" I ask.

"Well, you do appear to be the main character," my friend continues. "This is written from your perspective. See how every time a description based on your senses happens the word *I* is used instead of *he*?"

Immediately, *I* notice what my friend is talking about.

"Wow," is all that I can manage to say, the word falling limply from my mouth.

Treen is staring at me with a great concern now. "Do you even want to be pounded?"

I consider his words for a moment, glancing across the crowd and locking eyes with the muscular bigfoot before us who continues to dole out his white water rafting instructions. The second this brief exchange happens, a powerful surge of arousal shoots through my body.

"If it's him doing the pounding," I murmur under my breath.

Almost immediately, the handsome Sasquatch guide calls out over the crowd, pointing towards me. "Alright, you're on my raft. Everyone else, get into groups of four."

The crowd disperses and Treen and me say our goodbyes.

I stroll over to Garto to introduce myself. "Hey there," I offer, shaking his massive hand.

Garto's grip is firm and powerful, but his playful smile puts me at ease. "You ready?" he questions.

I nod.

"Let's go then," he continues, strolling over to the edge of the riverbank and pushing a large yellow raft out into the water. I help him along, and soon enough I'm climbing up into the floating vessel and grabbing ahold of a paddle.

As we begin our trek down the river I find an incredible sense of ease wash over me. I know this is only the beginning of our journey and that, eventually, this path will become wild and crazy, but for now I'm just enjoying the natural landscape.

"It really is beautiful out here," I offer Garto, who nods in return.

"Don't let your guard down too much," the handsome bigfoot counters. "But yes, for now, it's really something to behold."

Through the canyons we continue our float, with the rest of the rafts gradually drifting farther and farther behind us. Eventually, we round a corner and I realize that we've completely lost sight of the others.

"Are we pulling too far ahead?" I question.

Garto shakes his head. "These trips are personalized, every group has a guide to take them down the river, but they're free to branch out on whatever paths they want."

Suddenly, I notice a large fork in the streams up ahead, one of them continuing on straight while the other veers off in a sharp left.

"Speaking of," Garto continues, nodding towards the rapidly approaching bend.

"I get to choose?" I question.

Garto nods.

"Which one is better?" I ask him.

The handsome bigfoot smiles. "Depends on what you're looking for."

"Adventure," I propose confidently.

Almost immediately, Garto shoves his paddle into the water and veers us off to the left, our raft floating onward in a completely unexpected direction. Excitement floods my veins as I watch the fork disappearing behind us.

"This is so great," I tell the handsome bigfoot.

Soon, even more varying paths begin to sail by, flowing past us in rapid succession as we push deeper and deeper into the wilds of this enormous canyon. With every decision point I direct Garto towards even more adventure, and he doesn't disappoint. I may have been a little wary of this journey at first, but being guided along by my muscular bigfoot companion makes me feel nothing but safe and sound.

Along with the comfort, of course, comes another powerful emotion.

I'd thought Garto was handsome the moment I saw him, but the more time we spend together, the more this mild infatuation transforms into full-blown arousal. I can feel myself getting harder and harder just thinking about touching his soft, bigfoot fur, until eventually my cock is so swollen within my pants that it aches.

"Mind if we take a break?" I call out, mischievous thoughts of seduction suddenly making their way through my mind. "Maybe we can stop for lunch somewhere?"

Garto glances up at the sky above, then nods in conformation. "Looks like it's just about noon," the handsome bigfoot states. "There's a great spot just around the bend."

We glide down the river a short while longer, then eventually pull up onto the shore of a beautiful vista. This whole time, I'd assumed the canyon we were floating down was as deep as things got, but from our incredible vantage point I can see that there's an even deeper canyon stretching out before us. The view is absolutely breathtaking, and from this particular location you can make out the brilliant changing colors of a distant cliffside beyond.

"What is that?" I question, pointing over at the canyon wall as we pull our raft ashore and stroll up onto the beach.

"Various minerals," my bigfoot guide explains. "Over time, weather conditions and changes in the Earth's atmosphere created those separations of color. Meanwhile, the rivers were digging their way deeper and deeper through these rocks."

"Incredible," I gush.

"Definitely," the handsome bigfoot replies.

I can see now that Garto is eyeing me up, clearly on a similar erotic page. The attraction has been passing back and forth between us now like a feedback loop, building and building towards a powerful eruption. There's a growing lust that simply cannot be contained.

"I want you," I suddenly blurt, pulling off my shirt and tossing it to the side.

I step forward, pushing myself against the giant creature's muscular chest as he wraps his arms around me and pulls me close.

"You're so fucking sexy," Garto whispers into my ear. "I've been a guide for plenty of white water rafters, and you're unlike anyone I've ever had."

I look up into Garto's beautiful bigfoot gaze, then kiss him deeply on the lips as a shudder of aching pleasure pulses its way down my spine. We begin to make out with one another passionately, our hands exploring the chiseled topography of each other's bodies.

"I want to pound you so badly," Garto groans.

"I want..." I begin to reply, then stop suddenly.

Something inside of me has abruptly shifted, a strange emotional slant that takes me by surprise and causes my hands to completely cease their movement. I'm frozen solid now, struggling to determine what exactly is happening.

"Is everything okay?" the handsome bigfoot questions, deeply concerned.

"Yeah," I reply with a nod. "I just... this is so strange because up until thirty seconds ago I really wanted to fuck you, but now... I don't really feel like it."

Garto just stares at me blankly, clearly a little confused, but after a few seconds his expression changes to one of utter warmth and understanding. "That's okay," he says.

"Wait, really?" I question.

Garto nods. "I mean, it'd love to have a good pound, but your consent doesn't have a timeline. Just because you wanted to bang out this whole raft ride, doesn't mean that you can't change your mind right now. Hell, you could even change your mind *during* sex if you wanted. Then we would stop."

"That's very understanding," I inform him.

"Not really," Garto replies, shaking his head. "*Everyone* should know this. It's a given. If this makes me a particularly understanding bigfoot then that's a big problem, because this isn't something that's up for debate, it's just the truth. Your consent is yours to give and revoke at any time, for any reason. It's the business of nobody but yourself. Anyone who says otherwise is an asshole, and not the good kind of asshole."

I take a deep breath and let it out slowly. "Well, thank you."

"Don't mention it," Garto offers. "So, how about that lunch?"

I can't help laughing as the Sasquatch says this. "I wasn't actually hungry, I was just trying to pull off of the river so I could make my move."

"I'm not hungry yet, either," the handsome bigfoot admits.

I take note of my emotions, then finally continue. "I *do* want to spend so quality time with you, though," I admit. "Just because I don't want to have sex doesn't mean I'm not interested in learning more about what makes you tick."

"I'm in," Garto replies.

"I feel like we should go on a date or something. This view is beautiful, but I want to get dinner with you, maybe go to a bowling alley and throw some balls."

"There's a bowling alley right down the hill," Garto informs me.

"Wait, what?" I stammer. "Are you just fucking with me? We're out in the middle of nowhere"

The handsome bigfoot shakes his head. "This might be the middle of nowhere to humans, but there's a large bigfoot community in these canyons. Come on, I'll show you."

Garto begins to lead the way down the steep cliffside before us, taking a winding path of switchback after switchback as we make our decent into an even deeper canyon.

Soon enough, a small town starts coming into view, complete with a main street and a variety of local businesses. One of these businesses happens to be a bowling alley.

"See," Garto says, pointing. "Told you there was a place to knock some pins down."

Soon enough, the two of us find ourselves in the lobby of the bigfoot bowling alley, renting our shoes as a distant lane is assigned to us. The place is packed with several bigfeet in a variety of furry shades, from brilliant white to a deep charcoal black.

"This is gonna be a lot of fun," Garto tells me. "I haven't played in a long time."

"Not quite as good as sex," I joke, "but I actually *feel* like bowling."

"No better reason to be here than that," my bigfoot friend chimes in.

The two of us stroll over to our lane and start picking out balls, perusing the selections and taking a moment to test out the various weights and grips. At first, I have a bit of trouble finding what I'm looking for, but eventually a beautiful swirling purple and blue ball catches my eye.

I approach the ball slowly, placing my hand on its hard surface and getting a feel for its presence. I creep my fingers toward the holes but I don't slide in just yet, hesitating on the edge for a few seconds as I allow myself the pleasure of existing in this powerful moment.

Once I'm finally ready I slide inside with a deep, powerful movement, taking great pleasure in the way that my fingers fit within its perfectly sculpted body.

"How's that ball?" Garto calls from over my shoulder.

"It's incredible," I gush. "Wanna give it a try?"

The handsome bigfoot steps up and I hand my bowling ball over to him, the two of us still lost in a world of admiration for its rounded perfection.

"That's a solid ball," Garto confirms.

"Tell me about it," I reply with a nod. "Wait until you get inside."

Garto closes his eyes and then gracefully slips his fingers within, letting out a soft moan as they reach the hilt. Despite the fact that me and the handsome bigfoot have vastly different body types, our large hands appear to be vaguely the same size.

"You're lucky to have this one," Garto informs me, finally retracting his fingers and handing the ball back over.

I nod. "Ready to play?"

The two of us step up at a small podium, where my handsome bigfoot companion immediately takes charge. I watch as the beautiful creature begins to type in his name letter by letter, his huge pointer finger moving back and forth in slow, gradual thrusts. Faster and faster he goes, until his entire name has been spelled out and swiftly appears on the brilliant glowing screen then hangs above.

"More," I demand. "Do mine."

Garto winks and then immediately dives back in, falling into a confident rhythm now as his girthy finger pumps back and forth.

As I watch, an incredible realization washes over me. This experience that Garto and me are sharing is powerful, visceral, and important, but there's absolutely no sex. Still, we're finding the connection we so desperately desire in other ways, creating a meaningful evening that I'll never forgot.

When Garto finally finishes, he steps out of the way and waves me forward, motioning towards the smooth wooden lane. At the end are ten brilliant white pins just calling out to be bowled over by a perfectly placed strike.

"Let's see what you've got," the handsome bigfoot says teasingly.

I step up to the line, deeply focused, then launch my ball forward with one powerful swing of my arm. Despite the fact that I haven't played in months, my technique is perfect, and the second this bowling ball leaves my hands I know exactly where it's headed.

I step back and watch as the sphere careens in a slight curve, hitting the pins just right and causing a resounding crash to blast out across the bowling alley.

Seconds later, not a single pin is left standing.

"Strike!" Garto calls out proudly.

We continue to play through three whole games, drawing closer and closer as our session pushes on into the evening.

Eventually, however, we realize that we should probably get back to the river.

Being the gentleman that he is, Garto pays for the games, then takes me arm and arm as we stroll out of the bowling alley and onto the main street of this quiet bigfoot hamlet. Above us, the evening sky has transformed into a shade of deep purple, with hints of brilliant orange streaking throughout the clouds.

"That path back up to the river is this way," Garto says, pointing me towards the cliff.

The two of us begin our long trek back, but the buzz of excitement from such a fantastic date is still lingering within me. The erotic attraction that I'd been feeling for Garto has only doubled in its intensity, now consuming every thought.

Sure, I'd been certain about wanting to make love to him before, then quickly altered course, but something about this moment feels different.

Once we're a ways away from the prying eyes of the townsfolk, I grab my handsome bigfoot companion and pull him towards me. "I can't wait any longer," I gush. "I need you so fucking bad."

The next thing I know, Garto and me are passionately making out once again, our hands freely roaming across one another's bodies as surges of pleasure pulse back and forth between us. My hands are drifting lower and lower across the beautiful creature's perfectly sculpted chest, hovering at his waistband before making their final decent below.

I wait here for a moment, teasing Garto a bit, but instead of amplifying my arousal this moment only serves to cast doubt on the whole thing. Maybe we're moving too fast.

In this moment, my mind suddenly shafts. I realize that I'm no longer interested in having sex right now.

"Actually, nevermind," I offer. "Sorry to do that twice."

Garto shakes his head. "No apology necessary, just like our trip down the river, there's more than one path to take. It might feel like the inertia is pulling you one direction, but that doesn't mean you've gotta follow it. In fact, it's perfectly fine you just hop off the ride."

"But this is a tingler, right?" I continue. "If it's erotica, then the

34

readers expect a little sex. I feel like I owe it to them."

"You don't owe anyone a fucking thing," Garto counters. "And you don't need any reasoning or excuse for your decision. Who you sleep with and when you do it is your choice. It doesn't need to be qualified, even if you're a character in an erotica story."

I wrap my arms around Garto and pull him close. "I'm so thankful to be on this river with you," I say.

"I'm happy to be here," the handsome bigfoot tells me with a nod, "wherever the current may take us."

DRESSED UP HANDSOME AND NOT POUNDED BECAUSE COSPLAY IS NOT CONSENT

When I was growing up, it seemed everything I cared about just put a huge target on my back for bullies and scoundrels. While other kids were dressing up in the jerseys of their favorite sports hero, I was wearing the uniform of my favorite star fleet captain. I read graphic novels and played videogames, calling a comic shop on the corner my home away from home. I spent way too much time there, sometimes buying playing cards or models, but mostly just hanging out with the few like minded folks in town who seemed to understand me.

As I got older, however, a strange thing started to happen. Instead of my interests becoming harder and harder to enjoy, they've only blossomed into a worldwide phenomenon. Geek culture has transitioned from a tiny sliver of the popular consciousness, to an enormous economic juggernaut across every industry. Instead of being the only guy who cares when my favorite superhero finally make their way across the big screen, I'm part of the tidal wave of fans all struggling to find tickets on opening night.

For some people in my position, this has been a frustrating journey, but I don't mind at all. While I can understand the anger that comes with being ostracized for your interests, and then those interests becoming mainstream, I'm appreciative of the fact that I'm getting more exciting new content than ever. If others are late in joining the pack that realizes superheroes are fun and space travel is fascinating, then so be it.

Despite the rapid growth of this culture I love, I'm still in the unfortunate position of not being about to enjoy it much. With age comes responsibility, and a while I'd love to hang out at that old comic shop on the corner every day, I've gotta go to work.

It's more than a little overwhelming trying to carve out time for the things that I enjoy. Working in a stuffy office building from nine to five will chew you up and spit you out, and by the time Friday finally rolls around I'm just too tired to do much of anything.

This is why my initial reaction is a hard pass when my friend, Jorn, ask if I want to head into the city this weekend.

"I'm just too tired," I offer, sizzling hot plates of food sitting between us as we lounge in our favorite booth at the local diner. "I've been staying late at the office all week. I don't know if I'm up for a crazy weekend."

"I didn't even tell you what we'll be doing there!" my friend replies with a laugh.

I roll my eyes. "Fine. What's this little plan of yours?"

"Tinglecon," Jorn offers, the single word rolling off his tongue and hovering brilliantly in the air before him.

"Oh my god," I gasp, my entire demeanor suddenly shifting.

Tinglecon is a convention of like-minded folks who gather once a year in celebration of all things science fiction and fantasy that make you tingle with delight. They've had incredible panels and guest appearances in the past, but the convention travels around the country and has never once been close enough to make the trip worth it. There were rumors bubbling up about a nearby appearance of the convention, but I'd completely forgotten until just this moment.

"It's really happening?" I question.

Jorn nods. "This weekend."

"Is it too late to get tickets?" I stammer.

Jorn smiles mischievously. "It depends on if you have a friend who knew you'd wanna go." Jorn reaches into the bag settled next to his chair and pulls forth two tickets, placing them on the table between us so that I can bask in their glory. "Now, if you don't want one then I can certainly find someone else," my friend continues, "but I figured you'd want the first option."

I'm overflowing with excitement now, barely able to contain myself. "Of course I'll go!" I cry out, springing up from my seat and wrapping my arms around my friend. "Thank you so much. I can't fucking wait."

"You're welcome, Clippo," Jorn replies with a laugh. "Now all we need to do is figure out what we're wearing."

The second I hear this sentence my excitement kicks into overdrive. I'd completely forgotten about the part where we get to dress up as our favorite characters, arriving in style after crafting the perfect outfit. My mind is already flooded with various options, from a living corn to a bigfoot doctor lawyer.

"Who are *you* going as?" I question.

Jorn smiles playfully. "I was thinking about going as Gaygent Brontosaurus.

My eyes go wide at the mention of this notorious, prehistoric super spy. "That's a sexy outfit. Very sophisticated."

"Well, that's my style," Jorn replies with a laugh.

I'm not exactly sure which way I want to go with my costume, but upon hearing my friend's choice I immediately start pushing things in a sexy and suave direction. There are just so many options to choose from.

Suddenly, it hits me.

"I'll go as Darth Bater," I finally announce, landing on my favorite character from the hit film, Butt Wars.

Jorn nods in appreciation of my choice. "We're gonna have the best time ever."

As we drive towards the convention center I can feel my heart thumping harder and harder within my chest. On one hand, I'm excited, but on the other hand, I'm incredibly nervous. While I'm absolutely in love with my Darth Bater outfit, my chest and abs are completely exposed.

Don't get me wrong, I'm a guy who's proud of my body and have been prone to show it off, but right now I feel a little frightened by the prospect of revealing my bare skin to these thousands and thousands of convention goers.

Jorn notices the awkward look on my face from his position in the driver's seat. "Everything okay?" my friend asks.

I nod. "I'm just... a little nervous."

"What's up?"

I open my coat a bit to expose my bare abs. "Are you sure it's not too revealing?"

My friend considers this question for a moment. "Well, it's not too revealing for me, but it's not my decision. To be frank, it's not anyone's decision but your own. How do *you* feel about it?"

"I love the costume," I tell him, confident in my answer. "And even though it shows a lot of skin, I like that it's accurate to his outfit in Rogue Buns."

"It's very cool," Jorn agrees. "Well, if that's the case, then I don't think you've got anything to worry about. You look great and you did a really good job on your costume. If you feel like coming back to the car and changing into something else, though, just let me know and we'll do it."

Never before have I been so thankful for my friend, and his words immediately put me at ease. Strangely enough, I suddenly find myself perfectly comfortable in my own skin thanks to the fact that I know we've got an escape route.

Eventually, we find parking just a few short blocks away from the convention center and pull into an empty spot. We hand the lot attendant his outrageous fee and then begin our trek down the sidewalk, immediately joined by a horde of other convention attendees.

"Tinglecon!" someone cries out. "Let's do this! Woo!"

Various other walkers around us erupt with similar hollers of jubilation.

The longer we exist in this horde of other fans, the more at ease I become. Everyone is having a great time, and we haven't even arrived at the convention center yet. It feels like these are my people.

I feel safe.

The other encouraging thing is, for as skimpy as the outfits Jorn and me are wearing, there are plenty of others showing off an equal amount of skin.

"This is great," is all I can manage to say, the words rolling out of my mouth softly as a mighty sense of community builds and builds within.

Soon, the convention center comes into view, the crowd around us growing exponentially larger as we approach the front gate.

"Here we go!" I cry out as me and Jorn begin to make our way into the tightly packed gathering.

It takes a while but eventually we manage to squeeze through, show our tickets, and arrive on the other side of the security gate. Immediately, I find myself overwhelmed with the sights and sounds of nerd fandom, booths and displays stretching out as far as the eye can see in every direction.

I can't wait to dive in, but before we get started there's something that needs to be addressed.

"You go ahead," I instruct my friend. "I've gotta grab some food first, I'm starving."

Jorn nods. "I'll meet you at the Buttman booth in an hour," he offers.

We wave goodbye and then split paths, Jorn heading deeper into the convention center while I make a sudden right and begin my journey towards the dining hall.

I arrive and order a simple slice of pizza, not wanting to waste to much time on this meal, then find a seat at an empty folding table. I quickly dive in, scarfing the food down until someone abruptly stops me in my tracks by sitting in the chair next to me.

I glance over that them, melted cheese dangling from my mouth.

"Hey," the guy blurts, a reasonably handsome man dressed as a robot from some television show that I'm not familiar with.

"Hi," is all that I can think to respond.

There's something a little strange about the way this guy is approaching me, acting as though he's known me for years and I just happen to have forgotten his name.

"Do I know you?" I finally question.

"You can *get to know* me," the man offers in an unexpected reply.

The second the guy says this, a jolt of fear erupts through my body. To him, it's just another day at Tinglecon, but to me this is a moment I'll probably never forget. While the joy and excitement of this morning had given me to confidence to wear an outfit I might otherwise be uncomfortable in, I'm suddenly reminded of just how exposed I really am.

The man reaches out to touch my bare abs. His fingers creep closer and closer to my body as I freeze in a state of shock, but just as he's about to reach me I finally force out a single word, blurting it forth at the top of my lungs.

"Stop!" I cry loudly.

Immediately, the whole dining hall falls silent, the crowd freezing as they turn to look in our direction. The man who was reaching out to touch me has halted abruptly, his fingers hovering in the air just inches away from my skin. He wears a confused look on his face, not quite sure what's happening.

"What the fuck are you doing?" I stammer.

"Just trying to touch you," he replies in a strange daze. I can tell that this man is not very smart, the words falling from his mouth in an empty mumble.

"What made you think you could do that?" I question.

"Your outfit," the man replies, a long strand of drool dangling from the corner of his lips.

Before I can ask him any more questions, a team of uniformed security guards rushes over, grabbing the man and hoisting him to his feet roughly.

"We're sorry about that," the main security guard offers, a handsome T-Rex with rugged good looks and a sharp-toothed smile. This guard is slightly more festive than the rest, sporting a beautifully crafted superhero costume.

I read the dinosaur's nametag quickly. "Thanks, Gorty," I reply, struggling to maintain eye contact as the man reaching out for me is drug away behind him. "What was the deal with that guy?"

Gorty shakes his head. "It's not just *that guy*, you'd be surprised how common this kind of thing is."

"What kind of thing?" I continue.

"Men who think they have the right to touch someone or make rude comments just because they see another person dressed up in a costume they find attractive," Gorty continues. "It's an epidemic, really."

"Well, that sucks," I reply.

The handsome dinosaur nods. "We're out here on patrol, doing what we can. There's just a lot of this to deal with and we're stretched a little thin."

"What kind of guy would do something like that?" I continue.

Gorty takes a deep breath and then lets it out slowly. "Well, the men who assume someone else's outfit is a personal invitation to them come from all walks of life, but there is one common thread that ties them all together."

"What's that?" I question, overflowing with curiosity.

"They're all fucking idiots," the prehistoric creature informs me flatly.

I suppose this makes sense.

Apparently, Gorty can tell from my expression that I'm not entirely satisfied with this answer. "You wanna come downstairs and watch the process?"

I'm not exactly sure what process my new dinosaur friend is talking about, but I'm excited to learn.

"Sure," I reply with a nod.

Soon enough, Gorty is leading me through a nondescript door that places us in an empty white hallway, a far cry from the other hustling, bustling areas of this convention center. We're behind the scenes now, delving deeper and deeper into the mysterious world that keeps these huge gatherings organized and moving forward.

Eventually, we come to a door and push through it, finding ourselves in a small room with a few of the other security guards. There's a large window that faces yet another room, in which the man who tried to touch me sits alone at a table.

"Right now, we're trying to determine if there's any hope for him, or if he's just going to be a self-entitled moron for the rest of his life," whispers Gorty.

I realize quickly that what I'm looking through is an enormous pane of one-way glass. The man can't see us watching.

A scientist in a long white lab coat enters the room before us, holding something oblong and yellow in his hand. The scientist places this yellow item on the table before his handsy subject, who stares at it blankly.

From here, I can now see that the object is a banana is dressed in tiny slack and a long sleeve shirt, completely covered up.

"Now, you are not to eat this banana," the scientist instructs.

The handsy man nods with understanding, although it's hard to tell how much he truly comprehends based on his facial expression.

"You can do whatever you want when I'm gone, except for eating this banana," the scientist continues, making everything as clear as possible.

The man nods again, and with that, the scientist leaves.

Now the handsy man is sitting alone with his fully clothed banana.

From our own room behind the one-way glass, the security guards and me watch with rapt attention, curious to see what this idiotic guy will do now that he's alone with the banana.

The answer, however, isn't all that exciting, because the man does absolutely nothing.

Eventually, the scientist returns to the room, walking over to the table and collecting his uneaten banana. He then produces a second banana from his long lab coat, only this one is wearing nothing but a tiny pair of skimpy banana shorts.

"Alright, thank you for not eating the last banana, you did a good job," the scientist begins. "I'm gonna leave you with this *new* banana. Whatever you do, don't eat it."

The scientist abruptly turns again and leaves the room once more.

Almost immediately, the handsy man's demeanor has shifted. He's staring at the exposed yellow fruit with a powerful intensity in his eyes, a singular focus unlike anything I've ever seen.

It only takes a matter of seconds before the man reaches out and attempts to grab ahold of this delicious food.

"Ah!" he suddenly cries out, pulling back his hand and shaking it in the air, a futile maneuver that he hopes will relieve the slightest bit of pain.

"What's happening?" I lean over to ask Gorty, whispering the words under my breath.

"That banana contains an electric shock unit," my new friend explains. "Every time someone touches it, the voltage increases."

We watch as the handsy man continues to reach out and make his best attempt at grabbing the scantly clad banana that sits before him. Each and every time the man is seriously injured, to the point that smoke begins drifting up from his fingertips.

Eventually, security guards are forced to rush in and intervene before the handsy man seriously hurts himself.

"You see," Gorty offers. "They're all utter morons that have no understanding of personal space."

"So what's gonna happen with him?" I question.

"Well, he won't be coming back to Tinglecon any time soon," Gorty replies.

The two of us head out into the brilliant white hallway once more and continue our journey.

"So what happens if the subject *can* be rehabilitated?" I question.

Gorty seems a little upset by this query, clearly frustrated. "We're trying our best to figure something out," the dinosaur explains, "but the results have been disappointing, to say the least. Our scientists have come up with several methods, but most of the subjects are just too self-centered for them to take."

We walk in silence for a moment before Gorty finally continues with another suggestion.

"You want to see?" the T-Rex security guard asks.

"Sure!" I reply, thankful for an even deeper look at the inner workings of Tinglecon.

We walk a little farther and then eventually push through another nondescript door, revealing a massive room full of long tables and folding chairs. Scientists are sitting across from a broad selection of men, asking them questions and then jotting their answers down on pads of paper. There must be at least a hundred subjects being monitored.

"Each one of these scientists is explaining why the subject can't just go up and grab someone without their consent," Gorty informs me. "Regardless of how they're dressed."

"It seems simple enough," I reply.

Gorty nods. "It is, other than the fact that these guys are fucking idiots."

The handsome T-Rex begins to lead me through the crowd, walking down the aisles and aisles of men as we listen in on their conversations.

"But what if he's dressed as a mummy racecar?" one of the subjects is questioning. "That means he probably *wants* me to grab him."

"Why would you think that means he wants to be grabbed by you?" the scientist question. "It's just an outfit."

"Because mummy racecars are hot," the subject continues.

The scientist jots downs a few notes. "Nope, that's incorrect. Someone's attire is never an invitation for unwanted attention. Can you repeat that back to me?"

"Someone… someone's attire… some…" the subject begins to stammer, struggling to force the words out of his mouth, but the sentence simply refusing to form.

The scientist conducting this interview just glances back over his shoulder at us and shakes his head, clearly frustrated by the results.

Gorty leads us further down the aisle. "As you can see, we're at a bit of a road block with the majority of our subjects. Their feeble minds simply cannot seem to grasp even the most basic concepts that we present to them."

Suddenly, I freeze. An icy bolt stabs into my heart, stopping me in my tracks as a familiar face appears at one of the tables before me. It's Jorn.

"Oh my god," I blurt, nearly stumbling over backwards from the shock.

"What is it?" Gorty questions.

"That's my friend," I offer, pointing.

I run over to the table, interrupting their session in a state of utter panic. "Jorn, please tell me this is some kind of mistake," I blurt. "You're not really here for what it looks like, are you?"

My friend just shrugs.

"You know this man?" the scientist running Jorn's questions asks me. I nod. "I do."

"Well, I think he might be a lost cause at this point. Nothing seems to get through to him," the scientist continues.

I just stare at my friend, or former friend, in utter disappointment, not quite sure how to handle the feeling of heartbreak that creeps its way through my body.

The scientist shows me the top page on his clipboard, a long series of questions that are almost entirely marked with incorrect answers.

I let out a long sigh. "Dammit," is all that I can think to say.

"I don't even get what the problem is!" Jorn protests. "The guy was wearing a unicorn butt cops outfit. Obviously, he wanted to be grabbed!"

I throw up my hands in frustration, letting loose with an angry cry the fills the room. "What the hell is wrong with you? How is it so hard to understand that cosplay is not consent?"

The second these words leave my lips I notice something strange and powerful flicker across Jorn's face, a microscopic expression of acknowledgement that had been completely absent from all the other subjects.

"Wait a minute. What was that?" the scientist in charge of Jorn blurts out, jotting down a few more things on his notepad.

The scientist stands up and waves me towards his chair, which sits directly across from Jorn.

"Please, keep talking," the scientist says. "I'll observe."

I lean forward, looking my friend deep in the eyes and trying my best to connect with him on some basic, primal level. "Do you understand why you're here?" I question.

"Because the guy in the unicorn butt cops outfit asked me to grab him," replies Jorn.

I shake my head immediately. "No. He didn't *ask* you to do that. Did you hear him ask you?"

My friend shakes his head. "Not with words."

"Then how did he ask you?" I continue.

"With what he was wearing," Jorn continues.

"That's not real," I inform Jorn bluntly. "You fucking moron. That's not real."

My friend just stares at me blankly, but seconds later another strange expression of recognition crosses his face.

"What you did is *not good*," I explain. "In fact, it's assault. You can't just go around grabbing people like that, regardless of what they're wearing."

"I can't?" Jorn asks, looking more and more distraught.

Behind me, Gorty and the scientist are growing with excitement, clearly seeing a kind of progress that is rarely witnessed.

"No, you can't," I reply.

Jorn furrows his brow, clearly shaken up but this conversation. "Damn, I really messed up. Huh?"

"You did," I confirm with a nod.

"I'm sorry," Jorn offers.

I don't reply.

"Whoa!" the scientist suddenly interrupts, tapping me on the shoulder. "This is remarkable. Come with us for a moment."

I stand as Gorty and the scientist pull me aside, locked in a huddle now as we speak in hushed, yet excited, tones.

"I can't believe it," the scientist begins, the words billowing out of his mouth in rapid succession. "We've tried to explain it to these guys in so many different ways that we forget the most important variable. We forget to change *who* was doing the explaining. It appears that if a *friend of the subject* steps in and tells them what they're doing isn't cool, then the subject is significantly more likely to change."

I glance back over at Jorn, who is now staring off in complete silence. He seems very upset with himself.

"It appears that a powerful first step is for friends to let other friend know when they're acting like self-entitled pricks," the scientist continues. "It's not much, but it's a start."

Gorty is clearly thrilled with this news, turning to me with a huge smile plastered across this face. "This is amazing!" the dinosaur blurts. "Maybe with a little time we can integrate your friend Jorn back into society!"

I consider the head security guard's words for a moment, mulling them over while I struggle with the variety of emotions that flood through my body, the feelings mixing together like a strange and unexpected cocktail.

I take a deep breath and then let it out slowly, centering myself.

"Don't get me wrong, that's good news," I finally reply, "but Jorn's responsible for himself. I'll tell my friends when they're being jerks, but I'm more interested in doing that *before* they act, not after."

"I'm not quite sure what you mean," Gorty continues.

"I mean… it's nice that you've learned friends can break through to these people, but Jorn's not my friend anymore. It's okay if other folks want to pull their buddies out of the swamp, but I want to move on, and that's my choice. The person responsible for Jorn's actions is Jorn."

With that, I turn around and begin to make my way back to the convention hall. I'm thankful that Gorty and the scientists have found a solution, but right now I deserve to have some fun. I'm not interested in spending this weekend teaching jerks how to behave, I'm interested in treating myself to a good time, surrounded by good people, and proving love in my own way.

At the end of the day, what I do with my time, and my body, is up to me.

NICE GUY DINOSAUR DOESN'T POUND ME IN THE BUTT BECAUSE I'M NOT INTERESTED AND HE'S NOT ACTUALLY NICE HE'S JUST ANNOYING AND CREEPY AND DOESN'T RESPECT MY BOUNDARIES WHEN I TELL HIM WE'RE NOT ON A DATE

On days like today, it's nice to get a little sun. It's a warm, breezy afternoon and my friend Clamp and I are sitting out in the courtyard of my apartment building, grilling up some burgers as we relax on what it shaping up to be a pretty good Saturday.

Clamp is manning the grill while I'm lost in a haze, staring out at the lush garden before me and watching as large ferns sway gently in the wind.

"Did you hear about the Revengers Videogame tournament this weekend over at the comic book store?" Clamp questions, flipping one of the sizzling burgers as its delicious scent wafts across my nostrils.

"Wait, seriously?" I question. "That old school game from when we were kids?"

Clamps nods. "Yep, there's like a five hundred dollar prize."

"Holy shit, we've gotta enter," I blurt. "I used to be so damn good at Revengers."

"Already looked into it," Clamp informs me. "They had a limited number of entries and they're all taken. People bought tickets up to a year in advance."

"That's nuts," I reply.

Clamp finally finishes his work at the grill, pulling off our burgers with his metallic tool and flopping them down into a set of warm, golden buns. Cheese is already running down the sides of our burgers in beautiful yellow streaks, and a little onion, pickles, lettuce and special sauce only adds to the glorious sight.

My friend grabs two paper plates and carefully walks our food over, sitting the freshly prepared meal on the table before me. "This looks amazing," I gush.

Clamp pops open a cold bottle of chocolate milk and two of us toast.

"Thanks for having me over, Montan, this is fun," Clamp says as our glass bottles clink off of one another.

My friend and I both take huge bites of our burgers at the same time, reacting with shock and excitement at just how great these culinary creations have turned out. Neither of us is a particularly good cook, so this whole thing has been a welcome surprise.

"Remember when we'd play Revengers against each other on that snow level?" Clamp offers after swallowing his first bite. "What was that place called again?"

"Lockup," I reply.

Suddenly, there's a loud scoff from a bench across the garden from us. Clamp and I glance over to see a large green dinosaur in a black trench coat, chuckling loudly and rolling his eyes. He's got a fedora on his head and a bottle of bright green soda in his hand that is so neon I wouldn't be surprised if it was toxic to consume.

"Are you okay?" I question.

The dinosaur nods. "I'm sorry, m'buds. I couldn't help but overhear you talking about the Revengers videogame, a true classic for refined gentlemen."

Clamp and I exchange glances, not quite sure what to make of this dinosaur's strange attitude. I've seen him around the apartment complex quite a few times, but he always keeps his eyes down to the ground when he passes me. This is the first time we've actually exchanged words.

"What about it?" Clamp questions.

"That stage is not called lockup, it's called lockout," the dinosaur informs us, still laughing to himself has he shakes his head from side to side. I can see now that sweat is pouring down his forehead from wearing an enormous trench coat on this hot Summer's day.

"Oh yeah, I guess you're right," I reply.

"That's okay, it's an easy mistake for a casual gamer like you to make," the dinosaur continues. "Sometimes I forget that the world is not only made up of intellectuals like myself."

"Okay," is all that I can think to say, turning my attention back to my friend as we continue to enjoy our meal.

This interruption has thrown us so far out of our conversation that I don't even know where to begin again, at a loss for words.

As Clamp and I sit in silence, we begin to her heavy, labored breathing from behind us. We both look back to see that the dinosaur is still sitting in the sun, baking in the heat as he closes his eyes and continues to sweat through his coat.

"Are you okay?" I finally ask. "It's a little hot to be out to be dressed like that."

"Oh, m'bud. If you only knew what it truly takes to prepare for my gamer's battle you would not be so flippant with your words," the dinosaur offers. "I'm out here meditating as I prepare for the Revengers tournament tomorrow, clearing my mind. This is how I study the blade, and it's also how I'll study m'games."

"But why are you wearing a fedora and a tench coat?" I continue.

The dinosaur laughs. "You always train in the attire that you will don for battle, this is the Joker's first rule of war."

"I don't think it is," I continue.

"A gentleman gamer and certified nice guy like myself isn't going to show up at the tournament looking like a slob."

"Fair enough," I offer.

"I'm guessing the two of you are going?" questions the dinosaur.

"Oh no," I reply, shaking my head from side to side. "We just talked about trying to get tickets, but it's been sold out for a long time ago."

The dinosaur grins, then stands up and walks over to me. He reaches into his coat and pulls out a card, handing it to me proudly.

I read the card aloud. "Prenko Pimmis, professional gentleman gamer, pick up artist, and certified nice guy."

"At your service, m'bud," Prenko offers.

"Nice to meet you Prenko. I'm Montan and this is my friend Clamp," I reply.

Prenko doesn't even look at Clamp as I introduce my friend, his eyes fixed directly onto me. "You know, I happen to have three tickets to attend the Revengers videogame tournament, and I would be honored if you would go with me."

Clamp and me exchange glances. "Of course we'd like to go!" I finally blurt, determining that Prenko's strangeness is not quite bad enough to keep us away from some free tickets.

"Oh…" Prenko says, glancing back and forth between Clamp and me. "I only intended to invite you, Montan. This isn't your boyfriend is it?"

I shake my head. "We're just friends, I don't have a boyfriend," I tell him, "but we weren't super invested in the tournament so… if only one of us can go don't worry about it. Thank you so much, though."

I can tell the prospect of me bringing a friend really bothers Prenko, but is slightly more tolerable than me inviting a boyfriend.

Finally, the dinosaur accepts my offer.

"Alright, m'bud. We can all go, but you must promise to spend a large portion of the time with me," Prenko finally says. "I am a nice guy and I deserve to be recognized as such."

"I… alright," I reluctantly agree. "Just to be clear. This isn't a date."

"Of course. Meet tomorrow at five in the parking lot," offers Prenko. "M'carriage will be ready."

While some people like to dress up as their favorite characters for comic shop events like this, Clamp and I decide not to go all out. I'm excited to see all the cool costumes, but those take a lot of time to make and this is one of our first big videogame gatherings. Instead, I don a T-shirt featuring my favorite character and we head out the door.

When we reach the parking lot we find Prenko waiting for us, dressed in the same trench coat and fedora as before and leaning back against his car as he snacks on a bag of nacho cheese Doritos.

"Greetings, M'bud," he says to me as I approach, bowing deep and taking my hand in his. He gives my hand a kiss.

"Hey there," I reply in turn. "Ready to roll?"

Prenko nods. "You sit in front."

We pull open our doors and climb into the car, but the second I sit down in my passenger seat I notice something is very wrong. I turn in my chair to find that the entire back seat is filled with garbage, ranging from discarded snack packages to entire bags of Styrofoam. The smell is unpleasant, but even more concerning is the fact that there's definitely not enough room for Clamp.

"Oh, I'm sorry about that," says Prenko to my friend as he stands outside of the car. "I don't think I've got enough room for you."

"Should we just clean it out?" I question.

"No time," Prenko informs me. "The tournament is about to start. Your friend will have to find his own way."

Prenko throws his car in reverse and then pulls out into the parking lot, waving to Clamp as we drive away.

"He'll be fine," Prenko offers.

I consider making Prenko pull over, but then realize Clamp would probably much rather take his own car anyway. It's hard to tell which one of us is the lucky one right now.

"That's a nice outfit," Prenko offers.

"Yeah, I thought about going to this in some cosplay or something, but I'm new to the event scene so I don't really have any options. I wasn't prepared," I explain.

"Cosplay?" Prenko replies with a chuckle. "M'bud, as my date for the evening I would not allow your body to be exposed in such a way. I am a nice guy and I will protect the honor of m'bud, even if that means protecting him from himself."

"Sorry, but that decision has nothing to do with you," I reply, fairly disturbed already. "I just didn't have a costume made."

"Fair enough, m'bud," Prenko says, tipping his fedora at me.

We ride along for a short while and then suddenly Prenko mades a quick turn into the parking lot of nearby chain restaurant.

He parks, then gets out of the car.

"Uh… where are you going?" I question.

"I would never think to take a bud on a date without feeding him a proper meal, I'm a gentleman gamer after all," Prenko explains. "*Why do serious?*"

"I thought we were in a hurry," I retort. "Isn't that why you left Clamp behind?"

"A hurry to get to the restaurant," Prenko explains. "We're on a very strict timeline tonight."

I climb out of the car. "I'm not really that hungry."

"You can order as much or as little as you'd like," Prenko laughs. "I like a bud who watches his figure, though."

We head inside and meet the host, who directs us to our table right away. Prenko and I slide into our booth across from one another.

Every step of the way it has become more and more clear that Prenko thinks this situation is much more serious than it actually is. It's fascinating to watch and, although in similar situations I might be a little frightened by this clearly unhinged man, his extreme lack of personal care makes me think he's not capable of accomplishing much.

I decide that, for the time being, it's still worth it to hang out with this sad, strange man. After all, there's a fun event waiting for me at the end of the meal.

"You two know what you'd like to order?" our waitress suddenly asks, approaching with a papar and pencil.

"I'll have the chicken tendies," Prenko replies. "Actually, two orders of the chicken tendies. My friend here will have the salad."

"Right away," the waitress replies with a nod, then begins to turn away.

Fortunately, I have time to stop her.

"Wait," I cry out. "I have no idea why he just ordered for me. That's not what I want."

"M'bud said he wasn't hungry for much, and ordering for you is the gentlemanly thing to do," the fedora wearing dinosaur retorts. "Taking control is one of my pick up artist tactics."

"I'll just have a grilled cheese," I tell the waitress.

Prenko eyes me up and down for a moment, then finally shrugs it off. "So have to ever played Revengers?" the dinosaur asks. "It's a very complicated videogame. An intellectual gamer like myself can navigate it with ease, but it might be difficult for someone like you."

"Yeah, I used to play it a lot when I was a kid," I reply.

Prenko immediately breaks out in a fit of raucous laughter, trying his best to calm down but unable to do so. I take a long sip from my water, waiting it out until, finally, Prenko settles once more.

"You seem like such a casual gamer," he finally says. "I can't believe you've actually played Revengers."

"You already knew this," I inform him. "We we're talking about it in the courtyard the other day."

"I must have not been listening," Prenko continues.

"You literally interrupted us to have a conversation about it," I remind him.

Prenko shrugs. "I have a lot on my mind, especially after a good meditation or study session with my blade. I ponder a lot of advanced ideas that are difficult for most people to grasp. Questions about society. Questions about *real cinema*, before superhero movies were destroyed by wokeness. I am very smart, m'bud."

"Okay," I reply, just letting him talk it out.

Prenko continues rambling until the food arrives, at which point we dive in. The grilled cheese is actually pretty good, and the fact that Prenko can't seem to really talk and eat at the same time makes the rest of our meal considerably more pleasant than before.

When the two of us finally finish, the check arrives.

I pull out my wallet and put down my credit card, then watch as Prenko checks his pockets. "I'm sorry, M'bud, I seem to have lost my card."

"It's... fine," I offer.

The waitress comes by and we settle up.

Soon enough, Prenkon and me are heading back out to the car.

"Our first date, I shall remember this day for a very long time," Prenko tells me.

"It wasn't a date," I remind him.

The dinosaur seems to go out of his way to ignore this, because I'm damn near certain that he heard me. Regardless, he doesn't react, just hops in the car and waits for me to join him.

"Let's go," I offer as I climb into the passage seat.

We sit here idling for a moment, the car completely silent as Prenko stares at me with his huge dinosaur eyes, clearly waiting for something. I can see him from my peripheral, and I try to ignore his strange gaze for as long as I possibly can until, finally, I give in and turn to look at him.

"I have been a nice guy all night, and now you're disrespecting me," Prenko says, clearly a little upset about something. "You didn't even say thank you for dinner."

"Thank you?" I question. "I just bought it."

"I brought us here, though!" Prenko counters. "And I would've paid if I had my wallet."

"But you didn't," I remind him.

54

The two of us sit in silence for a moment.

Finally Prenko starts his car, still not saying a word as we pull back out onto the road. The dinosaur has shown me a lot of strange and unexpected emotions tonight, but now is the first time I've seen his simmering anger and aggression bubble up to the surface. His quietness is unsettling, but fortunately there are only a few blocks to travel.

It's not long before we're pulling up outside the comic book shop, where Clamp is standing by the curb and waiting for us.

We park, and Prenko turns to me. "Now, I have a few rules for when we're-"

Before the dinosaur has a chance to finish, I've opened the door and am climbing out onto the sidewalk. I give Clamp a big hug when I see him, happy to be around someone normal again.

"How was it?" my friend questions.

"Oh my god," I reply, my eyes wide. "I've got some amazing stories."

Prenko strolls over to us, clearly trying his best to remain calm. He forces a smile.

"Here are the tickets," Prenko says, handing one to each of us.

"Awesome," I reply, genuinely thankful for his generosity, regardless of how weird he's acting. "Thanks."

The three of us head inside, immediately greeted by a wild party of loud music and decadent foods. On a back wall of the comic book shop the Revengers videogame is being projected, patrons gathered around and cheering on the battle as it unfolds before them.

"Cool!" I blurt, finding myself a lot more excited to be here than I expected to be.

I turn to Clamp. "You want to go check out the game or should we browse a little bit."

"I might want to buy some comics, actually. It's been a while," my friend informs me.

The two of us head over and start browsing the neatly organized rows of comic books, flipping through them one by one and pulling out a few that spark our interest. We laugh together, joking about the covers and reminiscing over issues that used to be a part of our collections.

We're having fun.

"This is great," I say. "Hey, where's Prenko?"

We hadn't even noticed the dinosaur wasn't with us.

"Yeah, it's really cool of him to get us these tickets," Clamp continues. "Even if he is a little strange."

Eventually, we spot the fedora wearing dinosaur on the opposite side of the room, starring daggers as us as he watches in complete silence.

"Uh... do you think he's okay?" Clamp questions.

"I don't know," I admit.

Clamp and I wave at the dinosaur, who does nothing in return, just continues to stare back.

"I better go talk to him," I say, leaving my friend and strolling over to Prenko.

"Hey man, what's going on?" I question. "You wanna come browse the comic books with us?"

"You said you would spend your time with me here, now you're over there talking to some *other guy,*" the raptor says sternly.

"You can come hang out with us," I inform him. "We're not trying to ditch you. Besides, me and you already had a whole dinner together. I haven't seen Clamp all night."

"You probably like him more than me," the dinosaur blurts.

"I... um... he's a good friend of mine. We've known each other since we we're kids," I reply. "Do you really want me to say which one of you I like more? Because me and you literally just met yesterday."

Prenko begins to mumble under his breath, his words barely audible. "That's what I thought, just talking to Chad because he's handsome. He won't treat you right, though. I'm a nice guy, I'll always treat you well."

"What was that?" I ask, legitimately not quite hearing him.

"Nothing," Prenko replies.

"Okay... well, do you wanna come look at comic books with us," I ask again.

Prenko nods and then starts to follow me but stops halfway. "Just one thing," the dinosaur begins.

I turn back around to face the prehistoric creature. "Sure, what is it?"

"I'll only go if you promise you'll honor my nice guy points," Prenko says.

I have no idea what he's talking about, so I just stare at him blankly, not quite sure what to say.

Finally, I simply offer a single word in return. "What?"

"You have to honor my nice guy points," Prenko repeats. "I took you out to dinner, I've been a gentleman gamer to you all night. I even let you order a grilled cheese instead of the salad I wanted you to eat. That means at the end of the night you have to sleep with me."

"Are you... are you joking?" I question.

"I'm I gentleman gamer, m'bud. I don't joke about serious things like nice guy points," Prenko replies.

"Okay, I'm going to say this again and it will be the last time, because you ignored me earlier," I begin. "This is not a date. This *never was* a date, and it's never going to be a date."

"But, m'bud," is all that Prenko can think to say in protest.

"No," I reply flatly. "Second of all, that's not how it works. You don't earn points towards sex. This isn't some kind of a videogame, this is a real world interaction between two sentient creatures."

"But I'm a nice guy," Prenko protests.

"If you do nice things to earn imaginary points towards sex, you're not actually that nice. In fact, that makes you a horrible asshole," I continue.

I can tell that Prenko is upset now, literally trembling with anger. "You just want Chad!" he screams at me, causing the entire store to stop what they're doing and stare in confusion, not quite sure what's going on.

To be honest, I'm not quite sure either.

"My name is Clamp," my friend calls over from where he's standing. "Not Chad."

Prenko throws his hands up. "You owe me! You owe me sex right now for all the nice guy points!"

"You're disgusting," I finally say, losing my cool.

"I'm a nice guy," Prenko yells, "and I can't even get laid in a Chuck Tingle book!"

"Not everyone gets pounded in a Chuck Tingle book, because pounding is *never just a given*. It's about respect and understanding between consenting partners, and while there's a whole lot of things to explore within that realm, the most important thing to include is the *consent between partners* part," I explain. "Sure, we're characters in an erotica book, and sure, Chuck Tingle writes a lot about pounding... but guess what? I don't want to pound you, or be pounded by you. I don't like you. If that's not part of the equation then nothing else matters, and I don't owe you shit."

The entire comic book shop suddenly erupts into applause, clearly happy to hear someone say this to Prenko's face. I suddenly get the feeling that I'm not the first person he's done this too, that a dinosaur like this clearly has a problem understanding the boundaries of everyone he comes into contact with, not just me.

I can sense this is a turning point for the fedora-wearing creature. His mind is racing as the group around us cheers loudly, but where these thoughts are taking him I can only guess. Maybe this is the breakthrough moment that Prenko needed, a place on the timeline of his life where he can finally make a big change in the way that he sees the world.

Unfortunately, Prenko chooses to take the opposite path.

"You owe me sex! You owe me sex! I'm a nice guy!" the dinosaur begins to shriek with whiny belligerence, repeating the words over and over again as tears of anger stream down his face. "Fuck you! Fuck you! Fuck you!"

The crowd around us begins to boo, causing Prenko to finally lose his cool entirely. The dinosaur turns around and pushes through the door of the shop, his trench coat fluttering behind him as he heads out into the darkness of the night.

"That was… interesting," Clamp offers, stepping up beside me.

"Yeah," I reply. "I don't give a damn about Prenko, but I've gotta admit I'm a little concerned about the readers. Are they gonna be okay without any sex in this Tingler?"

"I think they'll get it," Clamp offers. "Sex isn't owed. That applies to everything, even erotica books."

I nod. "Let's get back to it then."

Soon enough, my friend and I are enjoying the party as it unfolds around us.

After an hour or so, I've completely forgotten about my strange confrontation, and it's only when the phone in my pocket starts to buzz over and over again that I remember Prenko.

I pull the device out and stare at its glowing screen.

"I'm sorry I was such and asshole, will you come meet me?" I read aloud, following the messages down. "Please respond. Please respond. Why aren't you talking to me? I knew it, you're just an asshole like I thought you were. Don't ever talk to me again, you don't deserve a nice guy like me."

Finally, one final message appears.

"I'm sorry about that, please call me," I read.

I turn off my phone and put it in my pocket, excited to spend some quality time with my friends.

NOT POUNDED BY THE PHYSICAL MANIFESTATION OF MY NEED TO PLEASE EVERYONE BECAUSE SOMETIMES IT'S OKAY TO GIVE BACK TO YOURSELF

I take care of people, and I'm proud of it. Whether it's during my time on the clock as a nurse, or when I finally get home and begin to process of helping out my neighbors with their landscaping, I'm here to give. It seems like I've always got something going on, and I feel like this does nothing but put a spring in my step.

Until it doesn't.

I'm on my lunch break at the hospital, making my way across the street to my favorite deli for a delicious sandwich, when suddenly I find myself feeling a little off. The sensation is fleeting at first, and it causes me to lose my balance slightly, wobbling back and forth as I struggle to pull it together. It takes a moment for me to regain my senses, and when I do I'm off and running once more, squarely focused on the Ruben sandwich that's about to rest squarely within my hands.

I get a few more steps before, suddenly, the dizziness strikes again. I stumble, me knees weakening below me as I struggle to stay upright. I can feel my vision going in and out of focus, and in a last minute attempt I reach out for the car parked next to me, struggling to find a reference point as the world swirls past.

Unfortunately, when I put my hand out for the car I quickly find that nothing is there, and the next thing I know I'm plummeting down towards the pavement with a loud thud as my whole world fades to black.

"Joey. You there?" comes a voice through the darkness, causing my eyes to flutter a bit as the syllables register within my brain.

"Huh?" is all that I can manage to say, the word barely slipping out through my lips.

"Good, you're back," the voice continues, becoming clearer and clearer with every passing second.

It takes every ounce of effort that I have, but I finally manage to push my eyes open and capture the light of the world streaming in. I squint a bit, taking in my surroundings and quickly realizing that I'm laid out in a hospital bed, back at work but on the opposite end of the usual equation.

My co-worker, Frenno, sits across from me, smiling.

"What happened?" I question. "The last thing I remember I was on my lunch break."

"You were, until you passed out on the sidewalk and had to be hauled back in here and hooked up to an IV," Frenno explains.

It's only now that I glance up and notice the drip hanging next to me, pumping liquid into my blood so that I don't pass out yet again.

"Not enough fluids, huh?" I question, beginning to diagnose myself.

"Not enough fluids, and not *nearly* enough rest," Frenno continues. "When's the last time you actually slept?"

I consider his words a moment. "Well… five minutes ago."

"Besides that," he continues.

I scan over the events of the last few days, taking note of the fact that last night I was out hauling firewood for a friend of mine until the early morning, and before that I was driving all night picking up two separate buddies from the airport at spectacularly inconvenient times.

"Now that you mention it, it's been about three days since I've had a full night of rest," I continue.

Frenno shakes his head. "You've gotta take it easy, man."

"I know, I know," I counter. "I'm just… I like to help, you know? That's why I became a nurse in the first place."

"That's great, it really is," Frenno explains, nodding in confirmation, "but you've also got to take a little time for yourself. If you're not healthy enough to help the folks you want to take care of, then what's the point? It's all about a balance."

"Doesn't that seem kind of… arrogant or something? Or self centered?" I question.

Frenno shakes his head. "You're important and special. It's okay to think that, because most of us need to be reminded sometimes. It's one thing to be self-centered, but it's something else entirely to stay healthy with a little bit of self love."

"Fair enough," I reply, understanding the sentiment behind his words but still not quite agreeing with it.

"Anyway, you'll be up and at it again pretty quick here," explains Frenno. "Besides the exhaustion, you're in great health."

I nod in understanding, thankful there isn't something more serious lying just below the surface.

My coworker stands and begins to walk away, but when he reaches the door he halts suddenly, then slowly begins to turn around.

"Hey, by the way," Frenno starts. "I'm part of a softball league, did I ever tell you that?"

I shake my head.

"We've got a game later today," my coworker continues. "I was just wondering, since you're gonna be better soon, if you'd mind helping me out and covering my next shift."

Covering Frenno's shift is the last thing I want to do right now, obviously, but there's a part of me that's unable to simply deny him. Deep down, I know that he needs my help and he wouldn't be asking if it wasn't an emergency.

"When do you need to me cover?" I question. "When's the shift?"

Frenno checks his watch. "In about… 5 minutes."

"And you think I'll be able to cover for you by then?" I continue, a little worried. "I'm still lying in this hospital bed."

"Yeah, but you're awake now, right?" my coworker says.

He's got a point, I guess. "Okay," I finally agree.

"Thanks man, you're the best," Frenno tells me, then turns to leave.

I lay back against the pillow behind me, now wondering how long I have to rest. Since the time of our conversation, a minute has probably passed, leaving me just four to work with. Plus, it will take a few minutes to put away the IV and get this room situated.

I suppose I should probably just get up now.

I rise and climb out of bed, pulling the needle from my arm as I go about my business. I have to admit I was really looking forward to getting home today, even before my big fall, but it's worth it to help out a friend.

When I'm finally finished, I head out into the hallway, but stop when I notice a swirling mass of potential activities floating about from the corner of my eye. I slowly turn to find myself face to face with the physical manifestation of my need to please everyone, who is strikingly handsome and smiling wide.

"Hey there," the sentient idea offers.

"Oh… hi," I reply, reaching out to shake the entities' hand.

"You headed off to fill in for Frenno?" the shifting physical manifestation questions.

I nod.

"Good! Awesome! Hey, I was just wondering if later tonight you'd like to watch that movie your buddy recommended to you. They one you said you'd watch and then tell him what you thought," the physical manifestation of my need to please everyone explains.

"I'm gonna be pretty tired after this double shift," I inform him while reluctantly sifting through my options, "but I suppose I could carve into my sleep hours just a little bit."

"Well, it's gonna be more than just a little," the physical manifestation admits. "The movie is four hours long."

"Four hours!" I blurt.

"It's experimental," the swirling entity explains.

"Then tomorrow morning maybe you can start watching the neighbors dog while he's on vacation?" this strange mass of responsibilities continues. "You know, filling up the food bowl, taking him for walks."

"I guess I'll have time if I don't sleep," I mumble.

"Great, great," the swirling mass replies. "Thank you so much for taking care of all this!"

By the time I finish watching my movie recommendation the sun is just beginning to rise over the horizon, filling my apartment with a warm dawn glow that would otherwise be very pleasant if it weren't for the fact that I just sat through four hours of the most boring entertainment one could possibly devise. In fact, calling it entertainment is pretty generous.

Still, I've reached the other side, and while I can't go back to my friend and tell him it was the best movie I've ever seen, I can *at least* say that it was a unique experience.

"Oh shit," I suddenly blurt aloud. "I need to feed the neighbor's dog."

I stand up to head for the front door when, suddenly, I find the physical manifestation of my need to please everyone blocking me.

"Oh, hey," I falter.

"Hey man," the physically manifested idea begins. "I saw you were just about to leave and I thought I'd let you know that you feel asleep during the first half of that movie."

"Oh… did I?" I question.

The swirling entity nods. "I just thought you'd want to know, so you can honestly tell your friend that you watched the whole thing. It would be a real shame to lie about it."

"You think I should go back and rewatch it?" I question.

The manifestation of my need to please everyone shrugs. "I'm just saying, you missed a lot."

"There's no way I can rewatch the whole movie, check on the dog, *and* get ready for work today," I explain.

"There's time… you can just call in sick," explains the physically manifested idea.

"But then I'll be letting my boss down," I remind him.

The manifested concept nods. "I suppose you're right."

It looks like there's only one option. I just need to work my ass off and somehow manage to fit it all in.

I'm not quite sure how I'm gonna do it, but I trust that I'll figure *something* out.

First thing's first, the dog.

Immediately, I rush past the swirling concept of my need to please everyone and make my way out into my apartment hallway. I aim straight for the residence of my friend, pulling the keys out of my pocket and readying them for entry.

I hit the door just right, pushing in the keys and turning them as some kind of hammering, imaginary clock pounds away within my ears.

The dog is immediately there to greet me, happy and excited as I fill his food and water bowls.

"Wanna go for a walk?" I ask excitedly as the creature bounces up and down.

I grab a leash from the table and soon enough my new canine friend and me are bounding down the steps of my apartment as the sky begins to bloom with a glorious imperial violet. It's another beautiful day.

Unfortunately, I don't have a chance to gaze at it for too long. Almost immediately, I pull out my phone and find a stream of the movie that I need to rewatch, jumping from scene to scene as I struggle to figure out what I might've missed.

It's a hectic walk, but I get it done.

"Nice work!" calls out the physical manifestation of my need to please everyone from the top of my front steps as I return to my apartment building.

"Thanks," I tell him.

"Hey, I was wondering," the swirling entity continues. "Would you be interested in going out on a date tonight?"

"With... you?" I question.

The sentient idea nods.

"I'm not sure," I stammer, completely taken off guard. "I guess I could fit it in."

"Sounds good, I'll pick you up for dinner after work," the physical manifestation of my need to please everyone replies.

The living concept turns to leave but I suddenly call out to stop him.

"Wait!" I cry. "I don't even know your name!"

"Crinn Sheems," he informs me.

By the time I've finished work and stumble out into the parking lot I can barely keep my eyes open. I'm feeling weak and delirious, but I'm trying my best to pull it together for Crinn. I promise him a date, after all.

Right on cue, the physical manifestation of my need to please everyone pulls up to the curb before me, smiling wide from the driver's seat of his beautiful white sportscar.

"You ready to roll?" he asks.

I nod.

"Hop in," the living idea continues.

I do as I'm told, climbing into the passenger seat and then suddenly pushing back into the leather as we peel out and pull away from the parking lot.

"Where do you want to go?" I question.

"I knew you'd let me choose," Crinn replies with a smile. "I was thinking Cheeseburgers."

I was in the mood for sushi, but it's fine.

We drive deep into the city, chatting casually as our destination draws closer and closer. Crinn seems like a nice enough guy, but there's something about him that simply won't let me relax in his presence.

When we arrive at the restaurant and head inside, I can only feel this nervous tension continue to build and build.

"Is everything okay?" Crinn questions.

I nod. "I haven't slept in like four days. Don't let that bother you, though. I'll be fine"

The physical manifestation of my need to please everyone nods in understanding as we reach our table and sit, pulling out some menus and looking over the delicious selection of burgers this place has to offer.

I'm not quite sure what I'm in to mood for today, but as my eyes scan the page in front of me I realize that it might not even matter. I'm so exhausted I can barely see the letters as they melt together on the menu, flowing into an incomprehensible mess.

"What should I get?" I question.

"Whatever you want," the physical manifestation of my need to please everyone replies.

"But what do *you* think I should get?" I ask.

"The buffalo burger," Crinn finally suggests.

I hate buffalo sauce, but I don't want to be rude and reject his recommendation after I asked for it.

Eventually, the waiter comes over and takes our orders.

"So what's it like being a living concept?" I question, hoping to get to know a little more about this handsome date that sits before me.

"Well… it's a little strange," Crinn explains. "Being a living concept is a lot harder than being a living object, because at least those already have a physical form. Manifesting myself like this takes a lot of work, you know? It's like… how is the physical manifestation to please everyone going to present to the word?"

"I like what you've done," I continue, making note of the little moving scenes that swirl in and out of his floating form. Each one of them seems to show me helping someone out as I suffer from the extreme exhaustion.

"Thank you," Crinn replies.

When the food arrives I suddenly realize just how hungry I really am, having skipped most meals over the last few days in an effort to help others.

Unfortunately, my excitement to dive in immediately dissipates when I remember what it is that I ordered. I hate buffalo sauce, and this burger is absolutely overflowing with the stuff.

"What's the matter?" Crinn questions. "Not hungry?"

Suddenly, all the tension that's been building within my body snaps, not outwardly, but with a deep internal weight that immediately dissolves around me.

"Hold on," I suddenly blurt, sticking up straight in my chair. "I don't want to see you anymore."

Crinn seems a little confused by this. "What?" is all that he can manage to say.

"I don't want to be on this date and I don't want to eat this burger covered in sauce that I don't like," I continue, simply letting the words flow out of me now. "I'm sick of putting everyone else first, and I'm sick of you."

"So like... you don't want to sleep with me later?" questions the living concept.

"Fuck no," I retort.

"Oh," is all that Crinn can think to say.

"For years I thought that putting everyone else's needs before my own was the right thing to do, and don't get me wrong, sometimes it is. But it can also be unhealthy when you forget to check in on yourself. I'm a really great person, and my time here on this Earth is important. I want to use some of it if for myself; *need* to use some of it for myself."

As I rant, I begin to notice that Crinn is getting smaller and smaller in his chair, the entity gradually dissolving as I accept the fact that it's okay to tend to my own needs sometimes.

"I want to eat where I feel like," I inform him. "I didn't want to go here tonight."

"Where did you want to go?" questions the physical manifestation of my need to please everyone.

"I wanted sushi!" I blurt. "But to tell you the truth, what I *really* wanted to do was sleep for like two days straight."

Crinn is so small now that he can barely see over the table, standing on his seat and struggling to make eye contact with me over the lip.

"In fact, that's what I'm gonna do," I continue, the physical manifestation of my need to please everyone disappearing completely into thin air.

I pay for my meal and stand up to leave, heading home.

Instead of taking one or two days off of work, I take a whole two weeks, deciding to use some of those seemingly endless vacation days that I've managed to rack up over my time as a nurse. It's only when I call in that I realize I've never once missed a day, and this realization proves even more that I've done the right thing.

Now, with all this time off, I've decided to finally knock a few things off the list of what *I* want to do for a change.

Having never seen the ocean before, the first step is booking a plane ticket for the Oregon coast. I make my arrangements for the very next day, finding someone else to watch my neighbor's dog and handling any other looming responsibilities I can think of.

During the course of all this, several friends have told me that I should find a part of the coastline with more sun, and I've quickly replied that I appreciate their input but *no thanks*.

I'm taking this vacation the way that I want to.

The second I land in Oregon, I know that I've made the right choice. This place is incredible, lush green trees and mountains stretching out in every direction as far as the eye can see. There's a powerful somberness to the mood, and unlike the beaches of California that are packed with lazy sunbathers, plenty of the sand here in Oregon is completely empty for miles and miles and miles.

I take a seat on one of those empty stretches of sand, hiking through the woods a bit until the thick forest opens up into a glorious view of the vast and seemingly endless ocean.

It's enough to take my breath away, and while I'd once imagined running down the shore and diving into the water, I drop to the ground instead. I sit here on my own, doing exactly what I want to do for a change.

As the waves go in and out, I find myself losing any bit of that tension that I might've still been holding within me. With every pulse of the waves

I'm reminded of the need for balance within all of us, a push and a pull that evens things out and keeps us healthy.

I should still help people out whenever I can, because it's something I truly enjoy doing, but hurting myself in this process is just not worth it.

Sometimes you need to prove love is real to yourself.

The second I think this, I notice a swirling figure making it's way down the beach.

"Hey!" I call out, feeling a strange connection to this mysterious being.

The figure stops, then turns to make his way up to me. As he draws closer I begin to notice that his body is made of several swirling images, the scenes playing out in an endless loop. Unlike Crinn, however, these vignettes are depiction of me taking care of myself.

"Whoa are you?" I question.

"I'm the physically manifested concept of your own self care," he says, "but you can call me Borgo."

"That's a very sexy name," I admit.

"Thanks," he replies. "I suppose I should thank you for willing me into reality."

"I did that?" I question, a little shocked.

The physically manifested idea nods. "Before this, you didn't really have much self care. You certainly *thought* you did, but in reality you were just wearing yourself down."

"And now that I've taken some time," I begin, "you've popped into existence."

"Correct," Borgo replies.

"That's pretty exciting," I offer. "That I can just make something out of nothing."

"Of course you can!" the living idea continues. "Haven't you ever written a song? Or a story? Or drawn a picture?"

"Not really," I admit, shaking my head. "I mean, it sounds like fun, but most of the time if I'm creating something then it's meant for someone else."

Borgo smiles. "I guess that's why I'm here then."

"To help me create?" I question.

"Is that what you want to do?" Borgo continues.

I nod, but instead of asking him any more questions I decide to take matters into my own hands.

CHUCK TINGLE

Abruptly, I turn around and head back towards my car, traipsing through the thick Oregon forest as Borgo follows closely behind.

"Ooo, I like this place," the physically manifested concept of my own self care says as he looks around the art store, his eyes roaming slowly across all of the blank canvases.

While these empty spaces would have once seemed daunting, like an oppressive task for me to complete, they now fill me with a strange sense of freedom.

I plan on purchasing a few of the canvasses, as well as a few paints and other supplies, stocking up on everything I'd need to create a beautiful work of art.

"What are you gonna do with all this stuff?" Borgo asks me.

"Paint the ocean," I reply. "I felt inspired."

Borgo glances down at the paints that I hold in my hand, then back up at me. "You don't have any blue, just so you know," the living concept notices.

"I know," I inform him. "I'd like to see the ocean as a nice deep red. That's how I'd like to paint it."

Impressed to with my confidence, Borgo just smiles.

I stroll over to the register and get in line to make my purchase, standing proudly as the excitement begins to flow through me. Blossoming creativity is such a unique sensation, and as far as I can remember this is the very first time that I've actually felt it.

I watch as the line continues to move along, the transactions between artist and cashier moving at a brisk pace.

I'm just about to the front of the line when the man before me falters, causing the whole thing to grind to a screeching halt.

"I'm sorry, but there's nothing I can do," I hear the cashier saying. "You're seventeen dollars short and we don't take cards."

The customer is clearly disappointed, but they don't put up a fight. Instead, they begin to turn around and place some of their items back on the shelf.

"Wait!" I cry out, halting the man in his tracks.

"I've got seventeen dollars," I inform them, then step forward, placing it on the counter.

70

"Thank you so much," the man in line before me says. "I really appreciate it."

Suddenly, I realize my mistake. Was this small moment of care for someone else going to bring Crinn, the physical manifestation of my need to please everyone, back into this reality? Would my new friend Borgo disappear from existence?

Fortunately, when I turn around I see that Borgo is still there smiling at me.

I pay for my art supplies and the stroll back over to Borgo.

"I thought you were gonna disappear," I inform him.

"Now why would I do that?" he questions.

"Because I paid for someone else," I counter.

The physical manifestation of my own self care laughs. "It's good to please others sometimes, just not everyone. Its all about balance, and what you did was very kind."

"Thanks," I reply.

"Now lets get painting," Borgo offers, taking some of my bags for me as we head out the door.

ABOUT THE AUTHOR

Dr. Chuck Tingle is an erotic author and Tae Kwon Do grandmaster (almost black belt) from Billings, Montana. After receiving his PhD at DeVry University in holistic massage, Chuck found himself fascinated by all things sensual, leading to his creation of the "tingler", a story so blissfully erotic that it cannot be experienced without eliciting a sharp tingle down the spine. Chuck's hobbies include backpacking, checkers and sport.

Made in the USA
Monee, IL
29 May 2021